INTERNATIONAL BESTSELLING AUTHOR
CASSANDRA FEATHERSTONE

Road To The
HOLLOW

M.P.P.

Copyright © 2021-2024 by Cassandra Featherstone

All rights reserved.

No part of this book may be reproduced in any form or by any electronic or mechanical means, including information storage and retrieval systems, without written permission from the author, except for the use of brief quotations in a book review. Any unauthorized copies will be pursued through DMCA, legal channels, and reporting to all appropriate companies and law enforcements agency, both foreign and domestic.

Contact the author for permissions or rights inquiries at www.cassandrafeatherstone.com

The characters and events portrayed in this book are fictitious. Any similarity to persons, places, brands, or locations—real or fictional—are coincidental and not intended by the authors.

AMAZON ONLY VERSION ONLY

Ebook/Print Cover: Little Tailfeather publishing
Alt paperback Covers: Pretty in Ink Creations
Editing, backgrounds, & Formatting: Little Tailfeather Publishing
Cassandra's logos: Pretty in Ink Creations/Artlogo
Goosebusters Alpha team: Kat Silver, Becky Ross, Denita Glenn, Ange Bennetts, Erica Taryn
Arc / Street Teams: Cassandra's claws, BCATS
Sensitivity Readers: Brit Mason, Gail Jericho
Translation Consultant: Mo Jacobs
Legal Services: Joshua Farley, esq.
Images/Fonts: Depositphotos, Shutterstock, & Photoshop

No GenAI was used in the covers or art within this book.

Stalk Cassandra Featherstone in the Dark Corners of the Web

Join my Facebook group and follow me everywhere!

Want More?

Sign up for my bi-weekly manifesto for a free series sampler:

Join my Ream as a FREE follower or exclusive subscriber to get access to cover reveals, WIPs, Serial Stories, and personal chats from me!

Content Information

This is a *paranormal whychoose romance with poly elements*—our FMC, Jolene, will not have to choose between love interests.
There are many situations included that are intended for <u>mature audiences (18+)</u>.
In this series, there may be instances/references (be they small or lengthy) that could trigger some individuals such as:

- liberal use of appropriate consent
- group scenes
- MMF, MM, MFM, MF, MFMMM, and more
- poison
- assassination attempts
- alphahole/possessive MMCs
- cinnamon roll MMCs
- slightly unhinged chaotic MMC
- unhealthy coping mechanisms
- extremely aggressive boundaries
- age gap (from 10 yrs to immeasurable)

- BDSM
- raw sex
- shifted sex
- traumatic childhood
- Alcohol use and abuse
- threats of bodily harm
- death
- body modifications
- fancy genitalia
- mate knots/barbs
- bullying (in person and on social media)
- PTSD
- blood
- emotional abuse from outside poly group
- body dysmorphia
- adult language
- pop culture references
- literary references
- emotional manipulation
- power play
- adorable nicknames
- physical intimidation
- emotionally abusive/manipulative parents (MMCs)
- voyeurism
- rough sex
- wings/tails/horns/magic in sex
- masturbation play
- markings/tattoos
- Easter egg character cameos from other series in the universe
- lawyers (ugh, but Jackson is a doll)
- family dysfunction

- super awesome BFF and her poly group
- animal companions
- absolute disrespect for shitty parents
- brief mentions of non-body positive dieting culture
- brief mentions of parental death
- very liberal re-imagining of history
- official corruption
- name calling
- occasional misogyny
- exhibitionism
- hand necklaces
- adult bullying
- magical kinks
- impact play
- elitism
- bribery
- corpses
- fat shaming (not by MCs)
- drama
- physical threats to FMC and others
- species-ism

No sexual practices in this book should be taken as safe or appropriate for real life application.

Content information is important and I don't ever want to harm a reader with inaccurate information.

Reader's Note
A few things you should know...

Road to the Hollow is **not** *a throwaway prequel*.

The world in which our characters live is set up in those books and you will be very confused if you do not read them. The series is planned to have six **whole** books and several **bonuses and gap novels**. I always recommend reading those because they often contain info you'll want later on.

This is a multi-book series, so *everything will not be revealed at once*. Some plot lines will continue through series in a larger arc and not get resolved in the first or even the third book.

I write lengthy books with intricate world building, strong character development, and *lots* of tiny threads that stretch throughout a series that may not always seem important at first glance. However, I promise nothing I put to paper and leave in the book is unimportant; it may simply become *more* important later on. There is no 'throwaway' detail in my worlds, so every scene will mean something eventually.

I promise it will all get tied up and have a HEA; don't worry!

Road to the Hollow is a why choose/poly romance, which means our FMC will not have to choose.

I would consider it a medium burn, slow build family group. It will continue to get spicier in the following books. If you're looking for porn with little to no plot, no judgment, but this isn't the series for you. It's also not closed door or FTB, so I believe the spice will be worth the wait. I realize spice scales are subjective and everyone has different opinions on it, so forgive me if mine and yours aren't totally aligned.

There are some characters and creatures that speak in other languages. I made the *translations clickable end of chapter notes* to help.

There are some words that are slang, jargon, or foreign that may seem to be spelled wrong—*please email the author or find her on social media rather than report to Amazon* if you think something is wrong. This has been proofed and edited *several* times since release; if you believe you found errors, you may not be correct. It could be a stylistic choice or a dialect choice. Please do not assume the two ARC teams, betas, alphas, and several proofers missed everything you believe is incorrect. Contact me if you find things; I want to make sure it doesn't get taken down so everyone can read!

If you see this book *anywhere besides major retailers or my website in ebook format,* please reach out to me via social media or email. Pirating kills my ability to write full time and I am so grateful for your help.

Contact Cass for issues or to report piracy: teamcassandra@cassandrafeatherstone.com

Author Ramblings

This new series has a very different tone than its sister series, *Codename*.

It's set within the same universe, almost parallel in time frame, but in a location from Delilah's past.

Our new FMC will have her own harem, her own mysteries, and her own series that will eventually intertwine with the inhabitants of the Rift in a third series (*The Ouroboros Society*) set after the events of *Codename* and *Misfit Protection Program*.

M.P.P. is a fast burn, funny series that will encompass both the current events and history of Deli's home town, Whistler's Hollow. There will be a lot of Easter eggs, but you can read *M.P.P.* without reading *Codename*.

This prequel, *Road to the Hollow*, is in Jolene's POV, but the first book *Return to the Hollow* will be told in multiple POVs. You will meet Jolene and some of the residents of this wacky, Southern small town, as well as the future harem members. You'll be teased with mysteries that won't be solved until later, and when you read it, you may only see HINTS about what the secrets the town and citizens hold.

Never fear, though, dear readers.

This is a PNR/shifter series, even if it doesn't seem like it at first. The mysteries surrounding Jolene's past and the infrastructure of the town will eventually reveal the truth.

If you enjoy this, please consider leaving an Amazon/Goodreads/Bookbub/Insta/TikTok review. The more buzz the series gets, the more likely it will be feasible to continue it!

Blood and guts,
Cass

To My Loving Family...

Thank you for supporting me by buying this book.

Unless you can deal with polyamory, sex, foul language, piercings, disrespect for authority, violence, and general snark about the world from a xennial and her millennial FMC, you should find a nice book with a beach and some lady's feet to read instead.

You'll have a more comfortable experience, and I won't get yelled at during family parties.

CAVEAT: If you choose to keep reading, know that at no time will I explain terms, positions, themes, tropes, or any other part of this novel at family events, in group chats, or on social media.

Don't ask.

CHAPTER TITLE SONGS

Road to the Hollow Chapter Playlist

BONUS PLAYLIST

Jolene's Bad Ass Bitch Mix

DEDICATION

This is dedicated to all the Gen Xers and Millennials struggling with the existential dread that is our memories of high school— all of the bullying, hazing, teasing, body image issues, and isolation has made us strong.

Jolene knows your pain, and so do I.

Mean Girls are the worst.

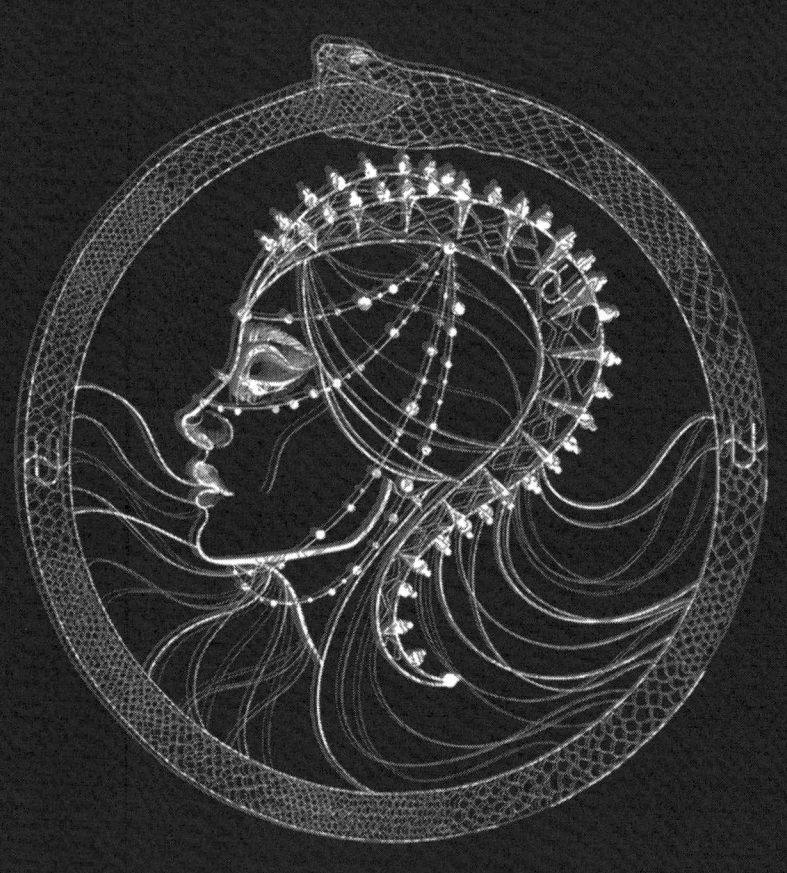

Home

"I'm sorry; could you repeat that?"

Looking at the agent in front of me in disbelief, I lean forward as if changing my position will alter the words that came out of his mouth. He grimaces, clearly unused to relaying this news to prospective trainees. After a moment of silence that feels oppressive, he clears his throat. I wait, unwilling to make his job easier.

"Miss... Whitley," he begins, pulling at the knot on his tie as he stands. He walks around the mahogany desk, coming to lean against the corner diagonal to me.

The crisp navy suit is standard government official, and the Harvard stripe on his tie tells me all I need to know about his upbringing. This guy grew up with a silver spoon in his mouth and rose up the ranks in the F.B.I. by playing politics. Handling a situation like mine is probably not his typical task, and I wonder why they chose him for this duty. I meet his gaze steadily, having learned the tricks of his trade from years of dealing with CEOs and officials with significantly more status than him.

He sighs, clearly disappointed that I'm not a blubbering mess. His wife—I can see the ring on his hand—is probably a sorority belle from UV that lets him run roughshod over her to secure her position as trophy wife. This man has aims much higher than his current position in the DOJ, and he's less than thrilled to be here speaking with me.

"Miss Whitley. As I said, I cannot release the information used to make hiring decisions. You can make a FOIA request, if you so choose, but I was told that because of the circumstances of your childhood, that request is likely to remain classified."

"Circumstances of my… I grew up in a small town in the Midwest, not Beirut! My parents were teachers, for the love of God. They have awarded me three degrees, and I developed a career consulting with governments and CEOs of multi-national corporations! I have NEVER failed a background check, Agent Grant. This is outrageous."

Crossing his arms over his chest, he sighs again, running a hand over his slicked back hair. "I cannot speak to that. I can only relay the information that we have denied your application, and that re-applying during another session will not change the results. You simply cannot work for the F.B.I. or any other agency under the Department of Justice."

I stand, infuriated beyond all reason. My eyes flash with anger as I stare him down. "This is *not* over, Agent Grant. I am *more* than qualified. There is not one blemish on my record. I deserve to be here. I will fight this decision tooth and nail—I have aimed all of my education and training at working within the behavioral unit of this agency."

Shaking his head, he pushes off the desk and drops back into the luxurious chair. "You can do what you wish, Miss Whitley, but the answer will remain the same. I suggest you focus your considerable talents and effort on finding another career path—one that is actually open to you."

My face is a mask of shock, but I quickly school it, picking up my purse and turning on my heel to stalk out of his office. I wasn't lying; I intend to fight this to the fucking Supreme Court if necessary. I've been working towards being a member of the profiling team since I left teaching, and I have every confidence that I can prove that I'm not only qualified, but in no way a security risk.

How *dare* they turn down my application and refuse to give me a reason? That can't be legal! It's a government position; they have to release the records if I request them. But the agent seemed to believe that I'd run into a brick wall with such a request, so there's something going on. Did I piss off some diplomat while I was in Europe and not realize it? Is someone pulling the strings to destroy my career?

I look around and realize that I've exited the building and I'm standing in the elevator to the parking structure. I was so angry that I made my way back to my car completely on autopilot. I check my pocket and realize that I even signed out and returned the visitors' badge. Taking a deep breath, I close my eyes.

It's been a long time since I was so angry that I had a functioning black out. The last time was when my parents got killed and because of my assignment, I couldn't come home for their funeral. The time before that was the last day I worked in a school. Both times, I lost time like this—I was functioning like a regular person to everyone around me, but when I came to, I had no idea what I'd done during that period. It usually lasts for weeks, but this time, it was only about fifteen minutes.

Clicking the remote to my car, I climb in and rest my forehead on the steering wheel. Each time this happened in the past, I spent months piecing together what happened while I was out. Through careful interrogation and immaculate people skills, I could recreate every minute of the lost time and record it in the journal I've been keeping since childhood. The school therapist always made me show her the journals to prove that I recovered my memories from the episodes.

Andromeda Bane was *not* a woman to be trifled with and even the kids and teens at the schools knew it.

I sigh. I haven't thought of her for a long time. The image of her powerful features and kind eyes fills my mind, and I reach up to wipe a tear from the corner of my eye. She clearly brooked no shit, but she was always available when I needed her. Her name was a threat and a prayer at Whistler's Hollow Formative and Finishing Schools. Those of us who grew up under her care defended her to the others—the ones who landed in her office because of intentional misbehavior rather than diagnoses.

My head lifts, and I sniffle, my heart crushed at what may be the end of my dreams. Perhaps it is time that I go home and face the place where my parents died. I haven't been there since I moved back to the States because I can't bear to see my childhood home without my parents in it. When they died, I used a state-side attorney to settle their affairs and hired a service to come in and air the house out every couple of months. I couldn't bear to sell it, although I never intended to return to the Hollow. It took my parents, and I never wanted to see it again.

But without the F.B.I. training, there's nothing for me in Richmond. I moved here when I came home from Europe so that I'd be in proximity to my dream, and if that truly is impossible, there's no reason for me to stay. Most of my belongings are still in storage despite living here for two years. I needed little creature comforts to work at the college while I finished my doctorate in Clinical Psychology online. I've been a nomad for so long that I haven't taken the time to develop relationships or put down roots here—even my lease is month-to-month.

It occurs to me I've been sitting in my car in the lot for a long time. If anyone walked by, they'd think that I've lost my marbles. I need to get home, make myself a drink, and think about this.

I never thought I'd be considering moving back to Whistler's Hollow.

Unfortunately, the past is no longer in the past.

Who Says You Can't Go Home?

Jolene

The living room is nearly done.

I've been slowly donating the things that I won't need. My forced career change has made some of my personal effects useless, and some things I left in storage necessary. I'll need everything I left tucked away to make my new life work.

Wiping my brow, I stop to chug the last bit of my energy drink. In most of the places I lived around the continent, I drank coffee in various forms, like it was the blood in my veins. Once I crossed the pond, the quality of my favorite 'go-juice' dropped immensely, so I switched to the much more American energy drinks. The sweet taste makes me sigh. It's not coffee, but it does the job.

My arms burn as I go back to stacking boxes in numerical order. I definitely worked my ass off today. I'll load up the last of the boxes tomorrow, and all I have left to put together are the items I will have with me in the truck. I could have taken a plane and hired movers, but I decided that rather than deal with lines and TSA checks, I would use the drive to prepare myself for small town life.

The smaller cities I lived in while I worked in Europe have a similar vibe to them, but American small towns are simply different. The customs, the people, and the way the community interacts are unique in every region. Despite having lived in Whistler's Hollow most of my life, adjusting to their particular brand of friendliness and venom will be jarring. I didn't have a terrible time in school, but I also didn't have an easy one. My parents weren't part of the old money, ruling elite, and those kids made certain that us commoners knew our place.

As an adult, I'm far better equipped to put a snippy socialite in her place than I was as a teen. It helps that I no longer have to worry about causing problems for my parents at work. However, since I'm running a small business and working part time at the school, I'll have to curb my instincts to squash queen bees. They knew me for my no-nonsense attitude in my former positions, but that won't work in the Hollow. The people there subscribe to the 'more flies with honey' adage, and I'll have to assert myself without ruining my ability to make a living.

Sighing, I rub my temples. I remember what the parents of my classmates were like. The few years I spent teaching in inner cities to pay off my degree was nothing like it will be at home. I left teaching because the lack of support burned me out, both from parents and the administration. Pursuing a career overseas provided me with the time I needed to finish my master's and make a comfortable living in beautiful cities filled with culture and history.

In the Hollow, lack of parent involvement won't be an issue. Too much involvement will be the issue. The administration will always side with the parents to keep their donors happy, so that problem will creep up as well. That's why I'm only working part-time—limiting my exposure. The rest of the time, I will run my gallery, make art, and give lessons to students of various ages.

Hopefully, doing that will keep the townsfolk from realizing my true goal. I'm not coming home out of nostalgia or to reconcile the estate. I'm moving home to find out what the hell caused me to fail my background check and fix it. If I learn anything more about my parents' death, that will simply be a bonus.

Whistler's Hollow won't know what hit them when I get done with them; that, I can guarantee.

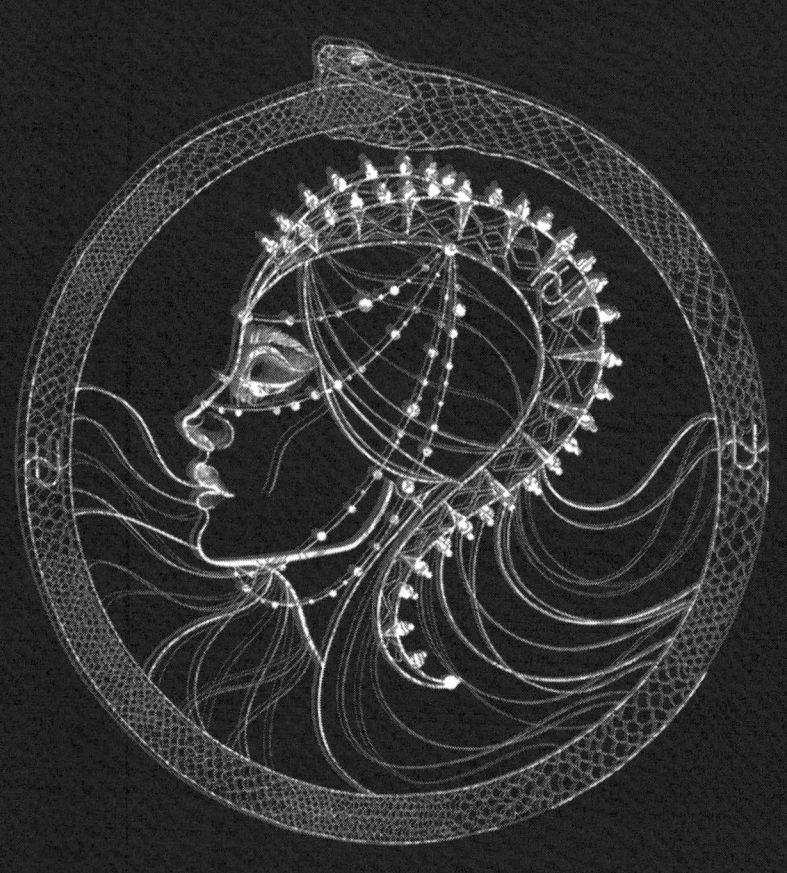

Take Me Home, Country Roads

Jolene

I may have underestimated the length of this drive in a box truck. Seven and a half hours didn't seem that long, but it's dragging.

The countryside is beautiful, and I didn't realize until I was chugging along through the rural areas of Virginia that I'd missed it. The lush greenery, the pastoral beauty of the farmland—it hit me right in the feels. I thought I'd become an urbanite through and through after all my years away.

I was wrong.

When I left for college, I vowed never to return to the small town, rural atmosphere that I grew up in. I was born to feel the thrill of the big city, and I thrived in its glory at State. I was even more cosmopolitan when I moved abroad, and the dreams of my youth got fulfilled by living in large, foreign cities with culture, history, and social scenes out of the movies. It felt like I arrived in the very place something destined me for.

Now, cruising past the fields and trees, the ache at seeing the quaint farms, fields, and country aesthetic makes me long for a time when I lived a simpler life.

Weird, right?

Maybe it's the passage of time—growing up, gaining life experience, maturity—making me nostalgic for a place that I swore I'd never return to. I didn't have the best experiences in elementary or high school, so I'm not yearning for glory days gone by. I'm not sure why my heart is suddenly having pangs of wistful familiarity with this scenery.

Whistler's Hollow isn't an awful place to live—don't get me wrong. But like many small Southern towns, there is a definitive hierarchy to the citizenry, and it becomes clear at a young age where you fit into that unofficial caste system. I wasn't at the bottom by any stretch, but I also wasn't anywhere close to the top of the pyramid.

The 'founding families' sit at the top, along with the town governing boards, and from there, it's a toss-up where you belong. I never understood the sociological construct that led to the social hierarchy, but it was clear who belonged where. After those at the top, it seemed like families whose parents held a 'position' in town came next—regardless of income level. So the town doctor, the vet, the lawyers were all in the next tier of regard, and after that came the business owners. Folks like my parents who were regular professionals fell below them, and at the bottom were the unskilled labor. I was never sure where some families fell as a child because they seemed to fade into the background since they didn't have children.

There were always a lot of children in the Hollow, and looking back on it now, it seems odd that the birth rates in my town were so high. I didn't pay attention to adults very much, so I don't remember a lot about it, but I remember a remarkable amount of baby and birth parties I attended with my mom.

I suck in a breath, my chest aching with memories of my parents. They were good to me, and though I didn't have the crazy, bonded relationship that some of my friends from college or my time overseas had, I loved them very much. They gave me everything I needed—within reason—and let me spread my wings and fly away when it was time. People were always curious about them not hounding me or visiting all the time when I was at State, but I didn't mind. I was ready to be an adult, and I appreciated they were willing to me do so without being as overbearing as some of my classmates' parents. We kept in touch, but all of my decisions were my own, and they always supported whatever I did.

As I drive in silence, I wonder if that's why I could remain detached enough to continue working when they were killed, and I couldn't make it home for the funeral. I'd separated myself from them so much as I grew older that my independence helped me survive losing them from afar.

Sighing, I ponder pulling off the highway for gas and a bite to eat. I have about four more hours until I reach the Hollow, and when I arrive, I have a mountain of things to do to get set up.

I have to go to the house and inspect the re-opening that the staff did to prepare for my arrival. I'll have to unload my personal items and get my living space squared away—a task that may involve sending furniture or leftover belongings that were my parents to storage. Eventually, I will have an estate sale or sell things online, but I won't bother until I'm fully settled in.

Once I finish at the house, I have to take the truck to my space on Main Street and unload all the gallery equipment and supplies. That will be an absolute nightmare because though I had the space inspected to ensure that it complied with all the permits and codes necessary to operate my studio and the display space, I won't believe that it's accurate until I go over it myself. It will take at least a week to unpack everything there, and another one to get it set up in the manner I prefer.

Whistler's Hollow has never had an art studio or gallery before, and to be successful in such a small town, I have to make certain that everything gets placed in a way that appeals to the sensibilities of the townspeople. The studio and lessons area will have to appear professional, yet homey, and the gallery can't be fancy and urban. Everything needs to fit within the mold of the American South without being overtly country bumpkin. The old Southern money in the town must feel at home, yet also feel like they are being very cosmopolitan at the same time.

It's gonna be an absolute bitch to design.

Shaking my head, I decide that it's time for a small break. Veering off the next exit that looks like it is a primary thoroughfare, I use one hand to query my GPS on my phone. It points in me toward a plaza with a diner where I can get some food, do some sketching on storefront design in my book, and hopefully, find a banging milkshake.

Milkshakes are one of my vices, and I can promise you I'm a connoisseur.

I pull into the back of the lot, using the spaces that trucks and vans gravitate to, and hop out of the cab. Stretching my arms and legs for a moment, I look around. This is definitely the part of town centered on business coming from the highway. The main drag is fast food, hotels, and gas stations—the actual center of town is further off the beaten path.

When my limbs feel solid enough to head inside, I reach into the truck to grab my messenger bag. It's made from an upcycled leather motorcycle jacket, and they sized the compartments perfectly for my phone, wallet, sketchbooks and pencils, and sundry personal items. It was a gift from the daughter of a fashion designer I worked for in Italy, and there's not another one like it on the planet.

I love it more than some people love their cars.

After I adjust my sunglasses, I stride across the lot and go into the diner. Smiling at the lady at the counter, I find the booth furthest from the door and sit with my back against the wall. It's my normal modus operandi, and I think it's because my parents always used to enjoy sitting in the corner where they could 'people watch'. I settle in, pulling out my supplies and arranging my workplace. Once it's ready, I pluck the menu from behind the napkin dispenser and peruse it.

When the server comes over, I look up at her with a smile that I haven't used in years. "Mornin', darlin'. What can I getcha?"

I sit the menu down. "You have an impressive selection of desserts. I'm a milkshake fanatic, and your flavor list is amazing. Is it a specialty?"

She laughs, her eyes dancing behind her long falsies. "Desserts are one of the best things we serve. We gotta line cook with a sweet tooth, and his creations are the talk of the town. You'll be happy with anything you order, sweetheart."

Thanking the universe for the intuition to stop at this exit with absolutely no pre-planning. I grin. "Okay. Then give me a pot of coffee and the waffles with fix-ins, bacon, and scrambled eggs. And I'll take the lavender pear milkshake, please."

"You got it, dearie. I'll tell Titus to make it all special for ya. I can tell when a gal comes from country stock, you know."

I chuckle, but this is exactly the behavior that wouldn't be out of place in the Hollow. "Thank you," I squint at her name tag, "... Darlene. I'm sure it will be worthy of your praise."

She scuttles off to place the order and help other customers, and I go back to my work. I open the sketchbook, turning it horizontal so I can start planning the studio space. I could absolutely use my tablet or laptop for this, but as an artist, I love to have tools in my hands before I switch to digital. All of my first drafts, notes, and other work start in sketchbooks and journals before they ever make it to my technology.

Once my food arrives, I sit the rough drawings aside, satisfied that I've got an idea of how I will set up the space in terms of furniture and equipment. I don't think I can truly assess what décor I'll choose until I can walk the physical layout, see what the town looks like, and absorb some of the current culture. Inhaling the scent of the delicious array on my plate makes me grin, and I dig in with fervor. I didn't realize that I was starving until now, but I wolf down the eggs and bacon in record time, only stopping to sip my coffee.

As I spread butter, syrup, and fruit on my waffles, I think back to my high school days in the Hollow. Most of the grads leave and don't return, but a select few come back to their roots and claim their place in the cultural hierarchy. Usually, those are the ones from the top echelon of the social tree, and they become as much part of the town landscape as the streets and stately homes in their neighborhoods. I remember a few of the graduates from my middle school years returning by the time I was ready to leave high school.

Eliot James Cantwell's father was a big shot that owned a sprawling horse farm just outside of town. He was headed for college when I was in middle school, and by the time I was a senior, he was back at home, taking over the business office for his dad. His twin sister, Fidelia, returned as well, opening a custom boutique on Main, right near the courthouse. Of course, it only catered to the wealthiest families and specialized in garments for cotillions and society events.

Percy Whitman Atwater came back, too, though I think he was a year older than the Cantwells. His family owned the grocery store, the farm that supplied it, and the acres of land used for many events, from farmer's markets to hayrides. He came back with a fancy business and agriculture degree but took a job in the mayor's office because his daddy wasn't ready to hand over the reins yet.

I finally reach for my milkshake, gasping under my breath at the sheer perfection of fruit flavors mixed into the concoction. Holy shit, this is the best milkshake I've ever tasted. I catch Darlene's eye as she bustles past and raise my glass as if to toast the chef. She laughs and winks at me, and I go back to slurping my treat like someone who hasn't eaten for a year.

When I finish, I pack up my supplies and drop the money for my tab plus a generous tip on the table. I wave at Darlene, so she knows to come pick up the check and head for the bathroom. I figure I should make sure I go before I head out, given that I want to make good time once I pull out. My plan is to drive the rest of the four plus hours straight through, and arrive in the Hollow about two p.m. That should give me enough daylight to get most of the house stuff unloaded before I must seek dinner.

I hit the head quickly, coming out to wash my hands and look in the mirror.

There are light circles under my eyes, underlining the whirlwind of activity that has been my world since the F.B.I. turned me down. I put together this move quickly, including shipping and packing my things from storage, and set up transferring my accounts and belongings to my hometown. There were a lot of sleepless nights and exhausting days that made it possible. My goal was to get home, get my life arranged, and start my investigation. I don't want to set off any alarm bells or let anyone in town know that I'm trying to figure out why being from Whistler's Hollow got me shadow banned from my dream career. Whatever the reason is, I can't imagine that it's a secret they want to get out.

Reaching into my bag, I pull out a scrunchie and pull my hair up. Since I came back to the States, I let the raven locks grow, and it hangs to middle of my back now. I haven't had hair like this since high school, and I'm glad that I did it. Looking similar to my former self will help me ingratiate myself with everyone. My green eyes are vivid in the dimly lit bathroom—they've always had an eerie quality that made them seem to glow in the dark. Obviously, they don't actually glow in the dark, but they're distinctive enough that folks will remember me.

I have to get back on the road. No more staring at the mirror and procrastinating.

With that, I head out the door and to the parking lot, determined to make the hours fly by.

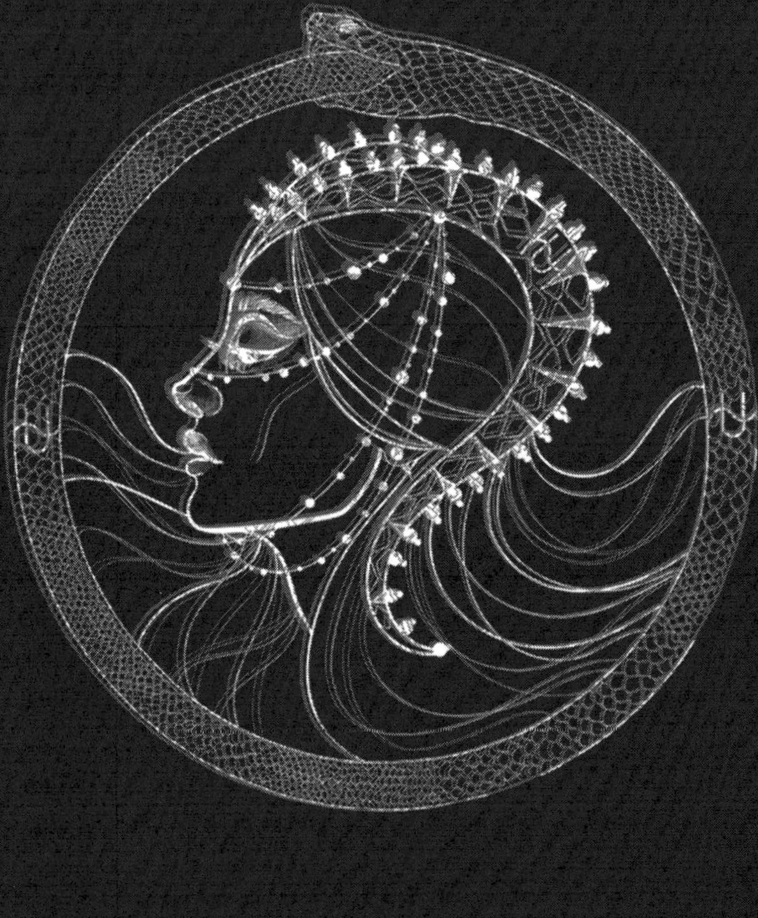

Life is A Highway

Jolene

Looking out the window, I groan at the bevy of colored lights in front of me. There must be a MAJOR wreck ahead because the entire highway looks like it's at a standstill. Once I slow to a stop, I glance at the GPS on my phone and let out another frustrated sound. It's *red* for the next hour of the trip map. Something terrible had to shut the highway down this thoroughly.

There's absolutely nowhere to get off and take a break, so I settle into the seat, putting the truck in park. I'm not going to move for some time according to the traffic notes, so I might as well troll the internet for information about the town I haven't even visited for almost thirteen years. I sip my soda as I flip through the search results, looking for anything interesting in the news first.

Nothing exciting, it seems. Some deaths, some elections, some town events—not a damned hint at what could cause my present issues. Maybe I should look up some people I went to school with. If they are on social media, I might get the scoop on the dirt from the Hollow. I've never been interested in their lives before, so I haven't even friended my actual close friends from my time at Whistler's Hollow Finishing School. Once I was out, I intended to stay out.

So now I have to open the major apps and start searching for the people I actually used to hang out with seeing if they have anything on their pages that will give me a clue. I frown as I look, puzzled by the complete *lack* of information available. The families in my town seemed to take pride in unique names for their children—we all lamented it as kids. It should be easy as hell to find Heathcliff Beauregard Standish—even if he's going by Cliffy still—or Annabelle Veronica Lee. Hell, I can't even find Delilah Lenore O'Hara or Heraclea Titania St. James and those have *got* to be the most extra names I ever saw go through WHFS. Of course, the last two were older than me, and since I was only a freshman when they graduated, I have no idea where they were headed when they left.

But I should *still* be able to find them on at least *one* of the major social media sites. Hell, who doesn't have an Insta at this point? Mine are all for my previous professional life, but I at least *have* the four major platforms to be found on. Why does it seem like none of the people I went to school with have even a minute online presence?

My lips curve. I may have struck out on the friendly folks, and even the older students, but I bet I can find the mean kids. There's no way that girls like Sherilynn, Amy, Jillian, Ophelia, and Reese aren't posing their kids or dogs or what the hell ever like models online. Those bitches made the bullies in movies look tame. They didn't target me specifically because I did everything in my power not to stand out. My family fell in the middle of the social pyramid, and keeping my head down meant that either side did not claim me. But I saw them target others, and their brand of torture was both terrifying and unique.

They have to be boring society mavens with dogs they carry in their purse by now.

I look up at the traffic, seeing not an inch of movement again, and then turn back to my phone. Typing in 'Sherilynn Grant', I find a few articles on charity functions—I knew it—and pictures that lead me down a rabbit hole until I find her Insta. As predicted, it's filled with professional grade posts of her house, her horses, her Italian Greyhounds, her very round and unhappy looking children, and her husband. She married Benjamin Louis Foster II—affectionately tagged as 'Benjy' in her posts—and I chuckle.

Benjy was dumber than a post in high school, but he was captain of the polo team, and his daddy owned a chain of diners across the state. It doesn't surprise me in the slightest when I can figure out that they dated through college—predictably. She was Alpha Delta Pi and got married once they moved home to take over Benjy's family business.

Oddly, Benjy himself doesn't have any accounts linked to hers, and he's only in pictures that she posts.

This is feckin' weird, my friend Saoirse would have said.

Sighing, I stretch my legs, putting down the phone for a few minutes. I miss my friends from my various assignments in Europe. We keep in touch here and there, but it always appears now that I live here, they don't have as much time for me. I never took the time to make friends in Richmond or in college because I was laser focused on my studies and my goals. I'm finding myself a little melancholy about it looking at the beautiful, curated lifestyle photos on Sherilynn's page.

I don't even have a houseplant, much less pets, a family, and twenty thousand goddamned followers. It wasn't supposed to *be* like this. I was supposed to be training at Quantico right now, finding my brethren in my fellow agents, and gearing up for the best job I've ever had.

Sniffling, I feel the first tears of frustration that I've allowed to fall since Agent Dipshit made his declaration in his office. I refused to let his adamant statement deter me, and ever since, I've been running full steam ahead to make it to my goal.

Hell, I'm not even sure what I'll *do* once I get there. I know how to set up my life in a new place—I've done that dozens of times in the past few years. But I don't know how I'm going to hunt down the nebulous reason that my application got denied. It's not like I'm some super sleuth; I'm an untrained profiler with a lot of background in psychology. The best I can guarantee is that I'll be able to read people well enough to know who to pursue until they let information slip.

That's it.

I grab a napkin from the seat and wipe my face, cleaning off the remnants of my pity fest. My parents may not have been the cozy, best friend types that everyone I've known has, but they taught me about grit and determination. My mom always said that the only way to get up from being knocked down was to be swinging as you brushed the dirt off. That's what I'm going to do. It doesn't matter if I'm not Poirot; it only matters that I have a goal. I can plan out the steps to get there and just work that plan until I see results or have to change course.

Picking up my phone again, I look for some of my male classmates. It *was* strange that Sherilynn is so active, and Benjy is a ghost. I'd chalk it up to the fact that he barely seemed to work doorknobs in high school, but he got some sort of degree. He must have at least learned to turn on a computer during that time. I can't believe that he's running a chain of diners—even with help—if he doesn't know how to work fucking Facebook.

My eyes squint as I try to conjure up names from my graduating class until I hit on the big one. Jesus, Mary, and the cuckold, I can't believe I almost forgot about him. The big kahuna himself, Edgar Olivier Boone III, *has* to be online. Captain of the football team, president of student council, valedictorian, captain of the debate team—Mr. Future Pi Kappa Alpha himself. His family is the oldest and richest in the entire state. They practically founded State U. When I lived there, his dad was running for state senate. There's no way that douche is a ghost online.

Fingers fly over the keyboard, and I gape.

Not. A. Goddamned. Thing.

At least, not in his own name. There are media mentions, pictures tagged by various people, and of course, an ass ton of photos of him with his dad on the campaign trail. Christ in a cartoon, the old pervert is an actual Congressman now. This fucking country is such a bloody joke.

There's Edgar—tormentor of fat girls, giver of wedgies, and pantser of band geeks—smiling like the beautiful, Kennedy-esque Ken doll he was raised to be. I read a little further down and my jaw nearly hits the floor. He's the county *judge* now? What in the actual...? That guy ran the biggest gambling ring on four counties when he was in school! He had adults coming for miles to bet on sporting events, both local and national. He didn't need the money, obviously. Edgar simply loved the thrill.

I mean, that's what I always thought. My observations from the sidelines were never verified, but I was certain that he was only doing it for the thrill of being bad. A little rebellion to help him bear the weight of expectations that his position in town put on him. I never shared that opinion with anyone because I had few close friends, nor was I part of that gilded inner circle. But I could see him straining against the bonds of his heritage in the things he did that weren't your typical asshole jock behavior.

We're all victims of our parentage, I suppose.

A car horn sounds behind me, and I realize that we're moving —a bit. So, I take it out of park and creep forward, still musing about the utter *absence* of info on some of the former Hollow students. It's pretty bizarre especially for the son of a U.S. Senator. When the movement stalls again, I stretch up to see if it looks like we're going to have to move again soon, and all I see is brake lights for miles. I've got time to dig a bit more.

Turning my attention to an adult, I try looking up my favorite counselor. Aside from a snippet on her credentials on the WHFS website, I find bupkiss. Andromeda Bane is not a common name, and I was sure that I'd find old Facebook pages or college stuff, but she, too, is clean as a whistle. I even try a reverse image search on her counselor picture, and it came up with squat.

What in *actual* fuck is with people from my town?

I had no idea that they were all such Luddites. It didn't seem that way when I lived there. People had cameras and took pictures —we had yearbooks. Is there something I'm missing? I didn't do a lot of social events and I kept my head down because my folks were teachers, but it feels like they purposefully left me out of some big secret.

Is this part of my F.B.I. rejection? Did the utter vacancy online of many of the inhabitants in my town make me suspicious?

Frowning, I try to think back on why I was so reclusive in school. The professors kid thing was part of it, sure, but I wasn't the only one. My parents weren't that active in the town scene, either; now that I'm pondering it, I don't believe that I ever saw them go to a party or event that wasn't for one of their colleagues or university donors.

As a kid, that didn't bother me—who wants to go to parties with boring adults—but it seems weird to realize it as a grown-up. Eloise Clara and Andrew Justin Whitley were introverted to the max, or there was something else going on. Grumbling under my breath, I type in my parents' names, my frustration climbing when I find a lone article on their accident in the *Hollow Hollar*, but nothing else.

This is fucking weird as shit, and it's not helping my paranoia about the failed background check.

Putting my hands over my eyes, I growl in annoyance at the situation, the traffic, and my life. UGH! I just wish I could get out of this fucking mess, get home, and start working on all of this bullshit. I slam my palm on the steering wheel and glare at the car in front of me.

Another horn sounds and engines start—*holy shit*, we're moving!

I crank up the radio, clicking my phone back to GPS as I inch towards freedom one car at a time. Within a few minutes, the flow is easing and I'm believing I might make it to town before dinnertime. Regardless of my research, I'm not ready for the town in large groups, and if I get there at dinner, I'll never be able to hide.

Time to push the limits of this truck. I gotta make up for lost time.

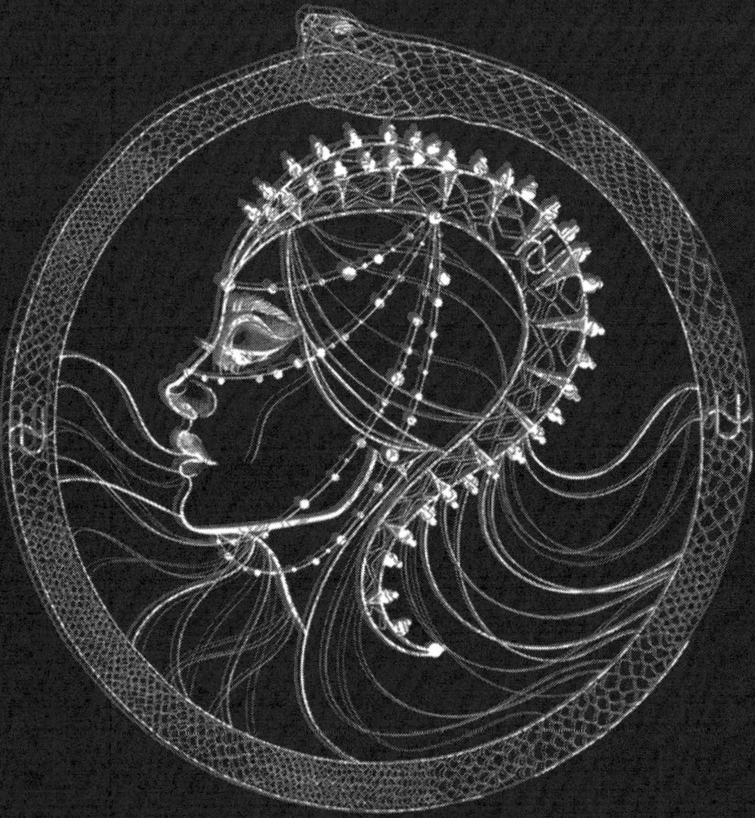

Welcome Home

Jolene

It's nearly four when I pull into the driveway of a house that I haven't seen in almost fifteen years. I hop out of the cab of the truck, shoving my hands in the pockets of my worn, holey jeans as I saunter towards the wraparound porch. The familiarity hits me, but oddly, nostalgia does not. I remember my childhood home, and I can think back on good times here, but no overwhelming emotion comes rushing at me like you read about in books.

Feeling vaguely unsettled by that realization, I walk over to the big oak tree that still has my rope swing hanging from a gnarled branch. I push on the board, testing that it is sturdy, and then sit down on it, pushing myself with my toes. My eyes roam over the house, and I wonder why I never realized that I was so detached from my past. I graduated, headed for college, and just... left. Being back should flood me with emotions and memories, but it's not. There's a blank spot where all that should be.

It's not bad, per se, but I know it's not normal. Nothing bad happened to me. They did not bully me; my parents didn't treat me poorly. I simply have no connection to this place or the people here. Thinking about it is like watching a movie about someone else's life. I see it all, but I'm not a part of it.

"Been a long time, hasn't it?"

Leaping off the seat, I whirl to face the person who sauntered up behind me and scared the shit out of me. "Holy hell!"

The wrinkled old lady throws her head back and laughs. "Sorry 'bout that, jellybean. At my age, I rarely get the drop on people."

I squint, inspecting her, and my face breaks into a smile. "Niecy! You nearly scared me out of my skin!"

She smiles indulgently, tilting her head as she looks at me from head to toe. "You always were a jumpy little thing. I should have remembered, but alas, the mind is foggier the older I get."

Niecy is the name I gave our housekeeper Bernice when I learned to talk. She and her husband Eugene worked for my parents and several other families when I was a child. They did housekeeping, grounds work, and light cooking for some of the finishing school staff so they would be available for school needs. I loved her peanut butter pie, and my mouth waters wondering if she remembered that tidbit.

"I kept the place looking nice with the help of my younger counterparts, just as Gene did the yard. After your poor parents passed and you couldn't come home, we followed the lawyer's instructions for care and maintenance to the letter. I always hoped it would mean that someday you'd return home."

Looking around for a moment, I take in the perfectly manicured lawn, landscaping, and exterior of the house. "You and Gene did an amazing job. I'm sure your 'extra help' comes from grandkids?"

Her smile widens again. "Surely does. I know Portia graduated when you were still in the lower school, but her kids are my dedicated helpers."

I frown. "Oz doesn't have any kids? He was older than Portia."

Turning towards the house, Niecy shakes her head, looking sad. "Come on, child. Let's get your stuff unloaded before it gets dark. I have cottage ham and beans on the warmer, fresh cornbread, and peanut butter pie."

The gasp flies out of me before I can stop it, and I give her a wry grin. "Foggy mind, my ass, Niecy. You're as sharp as a tack."

"Language," she calls over her shoulder, her voice laced with amusement. "You're never too old for a swat, jellybean."

My lips curve up as I follow the tiny woman across my yard and up the stairs of my home. I finally found something that made me feel nostalgic, and I'm going to soak in while I inhale the best food I've had since Europe.

○

Uggggghhhhh.

I ate SO much food, and it made Niecy happy as hell. Never mind that I'm too full to even contemplate unloading the truck tonight, and that's going to set me back at least a half a day. My belly is bursting with home cooked Southern food, and I'm not complaining a whit.

Groaning again, I roll off the couch and force myself to stand. I have to go get my bag and the duffel with my essentials. That way, I can wake up early and get a jump on my meticulously planned schedule. I'm already behind the eight-ball because of that traffic jam and my visit with Niecy. I can't let that spiral out of control. There's simply too much to do before the school year begins, and as always, I'm doing it all on my own.

I trudge out to the truck, opening the passenger door and

tugging out my gear. I'm so used to being on the move and having to travel light that I need little to survive for a day or two. As long as there's a bathroom and Wi-Fi, I'm usually good with just these two bags if I pack correctly. A shiver runs down my spine as I settle the duffel on my back, and I know distinctly that there are eyes on me. I don't know where they are, but someone is definitely watching me. Years of being a woman in large foreign cities alone have honed my early warning system, and it's never been wrong yet.

My cell is in the house. I didn't think I'd need it running across the yard in fucking Mayberry. In a proper city, I would never have taken the chance. But here? It did not occur to me I'd feel unsafe. I pause, pretending to root through my bag for something so I can buy time to decide what I'm going to do. I'm perfectly capable of basic self-defense—again, woman in big cities—but I don't know if this is a person or a stray mountain lion. The difference could mean a *lot* of surgeries—if I don't die. The hairs on the back of my neck tickle and a surge of what MUST be adrenaline courses through me, making my limbs feel tingly. It's a weird sensation—one unlike anything I've ever felt before—and I remain motionless at the truck as it flows through me.

I tilt my head, sensing confusion in the hidden watcher, and wait to see what happens. There's a whispered rustle in the foliage behind me, and as if by magic, the feeling of being spied on goes away. I frown, deciding a mountain lion or animal would *not* have simply yeeted off when I made myself a stationary target. That means that the eyes must belong to a human, and now I'm definitely freaked out. I gather my shit, slinging the bag over my shoulder as I hurry inside for the night.

Time to look into a fucking Ring or some shit.

Just fucking great.

When I wake up in the morning, I resign myself to hauling in the non-furniture items box by box.

I'm going to see if I can hire some local teens to help with the furniture once I have my smaller shit taken care of, but I want to organize as I go, so I haven't asked Niecy. She's so efficient that I would have had grandkids here at 8 AM banging on my door, so I waited. My compulsiveness about my space and how it's set up dictates I carry each box in, take it to the marked room, and unpack it before I grab another.

The first box is from the kitchen, and I open it, looking at the meager amount of kitchen tools and devices that I own. I've always wanted to cook—my mother and Niecy taught me well—but I never had the time or space as I moved around so much. Luckily, my parents' things never got packed away, so all the expensive dishes, tools, and gadgets are still here. I find spots for the admittedly slim pickings in my box, making certain to maintain the military-like discipline of my mother's organization system as I go.

After an hour, the kitchen boxes are done, and my stomach is growling like a lion at the zoo. I didn't have Niecy stock the fridge ahead just in case something delayed me, so I head for the bathroom to do a little touch up before I present myself in public. The Hollow was always a finicky place about appearances, and I can't show up looking like something a cat dragged in. It drives me bonkers, but this first re-impression could make or break my business prospects.

Eyeing my reflection, I tighten the high ponytail, fluffing the ends so it has bounce. I apply a little makeup—just enough to be presentable. My ripped jeans, three-quarter sleeve baseball tee that says 'Artists do it in colorful strokes' and worn combat boots would not be acceptable if people didn't know that I just arrived.

Trust me, *everyone* in the Hollow knows I've arrived by now. That's just how this place works.

Sighing, I check my bag for my phone and settle it over my shoulder. I walk to the wall, plucking the labelled key chain for my dad's vintage Impala off the key pegs, and chuckle. Man, the Winchesters would drool at his baby, and I'm sure Gene has kept it in pristine condition since his passing. I'm going to look like the worst news since the Civil War when I roll up to main street.

I kind of like that.

With a satisfied smirk, I head for the garage, deciding that if I'm going to live here again, I need to figure out the fine line between necessary Southern ass kissing and that old Yankee 'fuck you' spirit to survive.

○

As I swing into a parking spot on Main Street, I feel the eyes on me.

It might be paranoia, but the small-town grapevine definitely activated the moment I arrived yesterday, and people will check me out. I'm hardly the first person to leave the Hollow and not return, but now that I have, it's bound to get tongues wagging. I can only beg the Universe to keep every single person who approaches me from asking about how I'm doing since my parents' passing and commiserating about missing the funeral.

For one thing, I'm uncertain I've fully dealt with that situation myself, and secondarily, I can't talk about the reasons I couldn't return. The NDAs and official secrets type documents I signed almost daily while in Europe prevent me from discussing any of my work there. I've never breached that trust, so I know it's not why I flagged with the Fibbies. I'm not about to start with a Hollow-style Karen who wants fodder for the diner's dinner coffee klatch.

Climbing out of the Impala with my head held high, I adjust my sunglasses and sling my bag over my head. My shades are ultra-posh—a gift from a gadget guy that works for MI-6 during a brief jaunt in England—and I know the passersby can't see me assessing the scene.

The main drag of my former hometown has changed little: trees and clean sidewalks, picturesque businesses, and colorful banners on the iron work light poles. One end of the street leads into a renovated cul-de-sac in front of the city buildings and the other end bottoms out in the lots shared by the Formative and Finishing schools. They've done some polishing on the facades, but everything is exactly where I expected it to be.

I head down the street in the direction of the city buildings. The diner is situated kitty corner to the government structure. I'm sure much of their business comes from the employees and folks on their way to and from their jobs on Main. Through the protection of my reflective lenses, I scope out the businesses between the two massive landmarks on either end. There's a fairly broad assortment: a bakery, a furniture store, a clothing store, a toy store, a liquor store, a pizza place, a bookstore, the empty spot where my gallery will live, a bank, a salon, a doctor's office, a vet clinic, and a place with darkened windows and no sign. That one is odd, but maybe, like my space, it's under construction.

"Why, Jolene Whitley! Fancy meetin' you here!"

My brow arches as I take in the short, pastel clad man in front of me. I wholeheartedly disagree that it is a coincidence that the first person I run into on an early morning food run is Aldous Basil Longworth. He's been the executive assistant to the mayor of Whistler's Hollow since long before I was born.

His wife's family is part of the upper echelon of the caste system here, and he's always been an odious little toady. The years have been kind—or a surgeon has—because he doesn't seem to have an aged a day since I left. Aldous is still decked out like a Southern dandy ready to hit the Derby—pastel linen suit, coordinated bow tie/pocket square/shirt, shiny white Balenciaga's, and a jaunty hat.

I plaster on a fake smile, knowing that every word, gesture, and phrase will get reported to the entire diner by lunchtime, plus discussed in the hallways of the city building as I'm a Kardashian with a new sex tape. "*Bonjour*, Aldous. It has been a long time, indeed. I was headed to the diner to buy some breakfast, if you'd be so kind as to escort me while we catch up."

His eyes light up at the prospect of an extended conversation and he laughs like a high-pitched weasel. His hand places my arm in the crook of his and he pats my hand. "I would be honored, Miss Whitley. We rarely have alumni as illustrious as you return to settle in our fair town."

It takes everything in me not to shiver when he touches me. I'm not comfortable with strangers touching me after years of being a cautious single woman, and Aldous creeps me the hell out. When I was in high school, he spent a lot of time watching the cheerleaders' practices, and I've disliked him ever since. Plus, I'm not endeared to anyone who spends most of their life fomenting gossip and rumors and Aldous is the single biggest source of incorrect information in the Hollow. He'll repeat anything he hears without the slightest hint of validation, and its ruined reputations and lives aplenty over the years. He always escapes the consequences, though, because he works for the mayor.

At least, that's what my parents used to say when they thought I was in bed for the night. They thought Mayor Cornelia should cut him loose, founding family or not.

I have an entire catalog of those little snippets that I caught when my parents were unaware, and I think they will serve me well as I learn to navigate this place again.

"... don't you think, Jolene?"

Oh shit. I spaced out while the weasel was talking.

"I'm uncertain, Aldous. I've just returned, as you know." Please let that work...

He pats my hand with a creepy little smile. "That's true, dear. You'll need time to get settled into your home and that adorable space you've rented before you look for students. I'm sure that once you do, you'll contact Ophelia's Charlotte Marie for a prime lesson slot. After all, you were friends during your tenure in our lovely schools."

Again, I'm thankful for the special shades so this presumptuous shit can't see my reaction. Ophelia Jane Longworth was part of the upper caste 'mean girl' group, and I was hoping most of them had left the Hollow to marry old men for their fortunes. Hearing that she's here, has a kid, and will interact with me as a parent at both the school and the studio makes my stomach clench. But I can't correct Aldous because I don't know if he knows about her behavior and condones it or is like most of the men in town who don't have the foggiest what their spawn get up to besides things that win trophies.

"I'm sure that if Ophelia wants to put Charlotte in lessons, she will come to the open house so I can get her scheduled. Thank you for thinking of me, Aldous. It's very kind of you," I reply, keeping my tone bland. I don't want him to get even a tiny whiff of the disdain I feel for his daughter and their compatriots. After all, they are the people most likely to have kids and be able to afford pricey lessons or buy art for their homes. I have to be smart and sustainable while I get my business off the ground.

"Little Charlotte excels at EVERYTHING she does. She's in

the top ten percent of her preschool class, and was potty trained by the time she was eighteen months old!"

I blink, stunned into silence. What in the hell has happened to parents in the US while I was gallivanting around Europe for years? Is this a recent development or is it particular to the income level of a town like the Hollow? I left teaching to pursue my psych degrees because the parents and admin in my inner-city school were so disconnected from the success of the children. If Aldous is a good example, these people are *too* involved in their kids' success. Why would anyone in their right mind measure academic performance levels in preschool?

My bewildered thoughts are interrupted as the tiny man lets go of my arm and opens the door of the diner, making the bell tinkle. The din inside quiets as I walk in, and the eyes following me make the hackles on the back of my neck stand up. I paste on a fake smile, adopting the persona I'd left behind when I moved. Aldous follows me as I head for the counter, clearly puffed up at being the first person to locate me. I stop at the end of the counter, sitting on a stool as I watch the server clean up a place at the other end.

Aldous clears his throat loudly to my chagrin, the sound echoing in the diner like a socialite summoning a servant. This is *not* the impression I wanted to make on my first outing in town, and I certainly don't want to offend either of the classes occupying the diner. The server is mid-forties and looks comfortable in her skin, her sharp gaze slicing into Aldous like a hawk that's spotted a mouse.

"Aldous Basil Longworth. Do not make me tell you again. I do not appreciate the tone of your throat clearing when you get impatient, boy."

Holding back a snicker, I study this woman. I don't remember her, but since she's thirteen years older now, she could be someone

I saw daily. Anyone that makes a douche like Aldous shrivel in place is aces in my book. Before he can shoot the retort I sense is on the tip of his shrewish tongue, I hold my hand out, smiling. "Hello. I'm Jolene Whitley. I moved back to town last night, and I'm hungry as a bear."

A soft gasp echoes through the room, and I frown. What the hell did I say?

Her gaze sharpens again as she looks me over, and finally, her expression turns to a bright smile. "Jolene Whitley!" the server booms. "You are a sight for sore eyes! We didn't expect to see you return, especially with the stories your parents told us about your adventures in Europe. I expect you'll have to re-learn what life in the Hollow is like."

I look around, feeling the gazes of everyone in the room on me as I turn back with a broad smile. I hope it doesn't look forced, but with everyone studying me like a giant bug, I feel trapped. "I'm sure I will, and I know everyone in town will help me with that."

"Just come see ol' Hazel and I'll set you straight. In a town full of smiling crocodiles, I'm the friendly lizard of the group. Now, let me get you a menu..."

When her back is turned, I frown. Her analogy puzzles me, and I'm not sure the other people in the diner liked it, either. The hum of people chatting and eating starts again with Hazel's departure. I walk closer to the counter, noting a curious piece of artwork near the register. Art always intrigues me, so I lean into the sculpture of the Greco-Roman amphitheater with a backdrop depicting people dancing and a large green scaly looking icon under the stage. It's quite old, and I don't recognize the design, which is weird considering I did a lot of work in Athens. There's a small brass bowl at the forefront of the scene, and I chuckle. It must be her version of a tip jar picked up on some vacation or online with no thought to its actual purpose.

Hazel arrives just as I've liberated the few coins in my bag and dropped them into the bowl. Her smile widens and Aldous tries to cover a small gasp. Holy shit, is he that big of an asshole that he begrudges me tipping the server? What a fucking tool.

The server in question glares as the odious little git and hands me a menu. "Here you go, Miss Jolene. You take a look while I check on some tables. Aldous, you have somewhere to be right now, I assume. Mayor Cornelia isn't paying you with our tax dollars to idle in my diner."

His eyes practically drip venom. But Hazel just winks at me and heads for the floor to check in with the suspiciously quiet people eating.

"Well. She's an outstanding cook and has the best coffee for miles, but that *woman*..." Aldous huffs as if her lady parts had vexed him by existing.

"I like her. She seems very welcoming," I reply, not looking up from the menu. I'm hoping he'll follow Hazel's instructions and fuck off. I've grown tired of pandering to the little snipe, but I know that it's dangerous not to keep him happy. I'd like to get my food and head home in peace. I have *no* intention of inviting anyone into my home until I'm ready, and I feel Aldous might simply invite himself inside if he followed me.

"As the lady pleases, my dear. I trust you'll be happy in the care of our lovely townsfolk. Alas, our server is correct in that I must bid you adieu, for I have important town business to conduct."

Aldous looks as if he's going to grab my hand to kiss it, so I feign reaching for a napkin. "I certainly will, Aldous. I appreciate your time and your thoughtful escort. Please give Mayor Cornelia my best."

His chest puffs out, and he nods, turning on his heel to sashay out the door. A breath I didn't know I was holding whooshes from my lungs, and Hazel chuckles. She appeared out of nowhere. It takes all I have not to gasp. I hand her the menu as a cover, smiling a little. "I think I'll have the waffles with berries and cream, a peach milkshake, and if you have it, a large vat of coffee to go."

"Oh, I'll find something for you, dear. Moving isn't easy, and I'm sure Niecy will be by with more groceries later, but you need sustenance while you work."

I frown. "But I didn't ask her to do that! She doesn't have to—"

Hazel shakes her head and gives me a knowing look. "Oh, but she does, child. Accept it and move on—you'll both have an easier time."

My brows furrow, and I open my mouth to ask her what she means. But the server has skittered off again. She's surprisingly light on her feet, and I find myself alone at the counter while I wait for my order. After looking around to make certain that I'm not ignoring anyone, I reach into my bag and pull out my sketchbook and a pencil. I typically pass my time this way and being home won't change that.

I start by sketching the shape of her frame, getting the lines right as I watch her move about the restaurant. Hazel is solidly built, but there's a fluidity to her movements that makes her look almost serpentine. She glides through the tight spaces with ease, talking to patrons as she goes. Her ample curves make her look warm and matronly, despite the youth in her features. Her eyes belie her age—I could see the knowledge of her years in them as we spoke. In fact, it almost seemed like she was older than I initially pegged her, but based on her appearance alone, I know that can't be true. She definitely doesn't look lifted or tucked, as many of the wives in town will when I see them again. It's a bit of a mystery, though I suppose good genes trump all.

"Excuse me. I hate to interrupt, but I've been told that you're the new equestrian in town."

I turn to look at the person who tapped on my shoulder and I drop my pencil, watching it clatter to the ground like a fool. I can't seem to move, and my mouth is hanging open far enough to catch flies, as Niecy would say. "I... uh..."

The stranger grins, his smile like sunshine on a rainy day. His brilliant white teeth, full lips and sapphire eyes have me completely stymied. Bending down, he picks up the pencil and reaches up to hand it to me. The pose looks like a proposal and my face flames red as I take it. Once he stands again, he tilts his head, eyes dancing with merriment. "I'm Wolfgang Fletcher. My friends call me Wolfie."

My mouth opens and closes again as I take in the formfitting jeans, tight white tee, and leather jacket. He's clearly a decade younger than me, and I feel like a creeper being so instantly attracted to him. "I'm... I'm uh, Jolene. Jolene Whitley."

His chuckle is adorable, and he winks. "I know. I was younger than you, for sure, but I grew up here. I'm the town vet."

I blink. "Holy hell. Aren't you young to be graduated from vet school?"

"I graduated early from undergrad. I'm... well, I'm pretty smart," he says, rubbing the back of his neck.

Hazel walks up with a to-go bag and a huge thermos, harrumphing under her breath. "He's a damned genius is what he is. Don't let him pull that humble good old boy routine on you. Wolfgang Lucien Fletcher, you be honest with Jolene."

"Aw, Haze, I wasn't lying. You know I don't like to say that to people. Everyone looks at me like I'm some kind of a freak as it is." The hot guy whines to my food carrying savior like they're old friends, and the contrast between his behavior and Aldous' couldn't be more striking.

"It's okay. Asking your IQ is more of a first date question, anyway."

They both go quiet, and I smack myself in the face, cringing as I hit my nose. I'm fucking amazing with diplomats and despots, but I am USELESS with dating. I quit trying a long time ago. I simply make friends to enjoy their company and have escorts to events, but nothing more comes of it. I've resigned myself to becoming a cat lady soon.

"That sounds like an invitation, Jolene Whitley. Whether you meant to say that out loud, I'm going to take it. Perhaps we could have lunch at the ranch on Friday, and I'll introduce you to the horses?"

"She'd love to," Hazel says, giving me a look that says I don't have an option.

I'm completely speechless again as the two of them look at me expectantly. "I, um, yes. Yes, that would be nice. I would like to meet the horses."

Hot, young 'Wolfie' guy beams and holds his hand out. "Hand me your phone, and I'll put my info in."

I nod, obeying like a good little automaton. My eyes narrow as I look at Hazel, but she just grins like a Cheshire Cat. Meddling people... *that's* one thing I didn't miss about small-town life.

"Okay, I'm good. You better head out before your food gets cold. I'm sure you lots to do before lunch," Wolfie says.

Nodding again, I try to smile and not look like a full-on moron. "Yes. I do. Um, thank you, Hazel. I'll, um, see you... later."

I snatch the bag and the thermos and practically run out of the dinner back to the Impala.

What in the *hell* just happened?

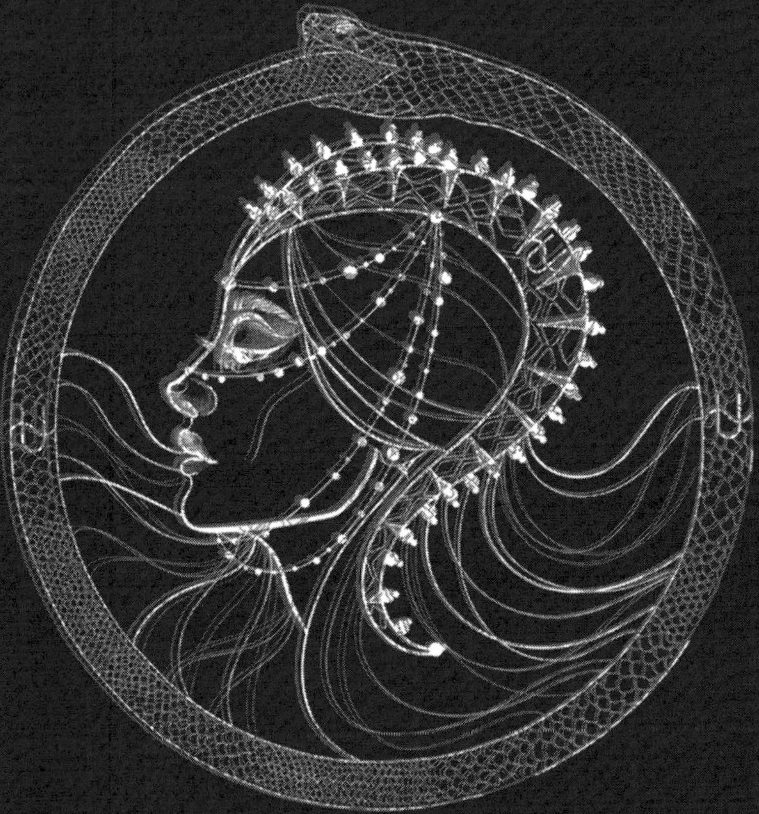

Proud Mary

Jolene

When I get home, I'm relieved to find that no one is waiting on my doorstep like a kid at a zoo exhibit. Given Aldous' immediately latching on and the hottie vet, I'm peopled out for a while. I don't mean that in an 'I'm an introvert; I need to re-charge' kind of way; I just have shit to do, and if I don't get it done, I'm going to have trouble staying on schedule.

I *hate* feeling rushed.

Dumping my shit on the kitchen island, I pull out my sketchbook to finish the line art for my drawing while I eat. I'm pleasantly surprised by quality of the waffles and the milkshake—I wonder if Hazel would be open to trying more adventurous flavors? I sketch as I muse on flavor combos to suggest, and I get so absorbed that I almost miss the front door opening.

Almost.

"Who's there?" I call, rising to my feet. Remembering the eyes from the night before, I tiptoe on bare feet to my bag, pulling the spiked brass knuckles out of the front pocket in a practiced motion. No one answers, so I creep towards the living room, staying behind corners and in blind spots until I'm sure there's no one waiting for me on the other side. When I get to the living room, I look from left to right nervously, and a *thump* makes me jump three feet in the air.

"Holy Shit!" Looking around in full panic mode, I curl my hands in brass knuckled fists and get ready to defend myself.

Another thump is followed by a vase crashing to the ground and a large animal leaping towards me like a predator in a Discovery Channel show.

What the fuck?!

"Ooooooof!" I grunt, falling backwards onto the hardwood in a heap. A low rumble vibrates over me as the animal stands on my chest, making it impossible to catch my breath. An answering yowl echoes from upstairs, and before I know it, another monster joins the one pinning me. It looks down at me curiously, its furry face upside down over mine.

I'm being attacked by two gorgeous, full grown serval cats.

Where in the *hell* did these beasts come from?

These things cost a *fortune*, and usually, owners keep them close for fear of them terrorizing local wildlife. The one on top of me leans down and licks my face from top to bottom and the one above me makes another yowling sound. I reach up carefully—they ARE wild animals, even if someone is keeping them as pets—and scritch the heavy chest smasher behind the ears.

"Who do you belong to, buddy? You're too pretty to be roaming my house like a lost kitten."

The cats yowl in response, which tells me they're definitely used to humans. Cats only meow to humans, and these guys are much more feral than a house cat. Unfortunately, that doesn't help me puzzle out who they belong to. Neither have collars nor obvious chip bumps I can see.

Whistler's Hollow is a *weird* fucking town.

After a few more minutes, I finally move, adjusting the perched cat to the floor so I can get up. When I stand, they both look at me as if waiting for a command. I wrinkle my nose, unsure of what to do. We never had pets growing up and hell if I know what I'm supposed to when someone's wild animals break into my house. Giving them a stern look, I point at one and then the other. "Go home!"

They look at me, then each other, and trot over to the ugly, floral couch my mother loved so much. In a second, they're perched on it, sprawled out like a Nat Geo photo shoot.

What the goddamned hell? This is *not* their home. Do they not know that command? Maybe they only know commands in another language? I knew several Yard boys in England whose K9s responded to orders in German. Could that be why they got confused?

"Okay, fine, guys. You can stay there. I'm going to put that ugly thing in storage for the estate sale, anyway. I don't have time to figure out if you only know Cajun French or whatever. Hang out if you want—I have to go to the truck to bring in the stuff for the laundry room."

The beautiful cats simply blink at me, content to lounge where they are.

Jesus H. Tap Dancing Christ.

○

Looking out the window at the setting sun, I sigh.

Despite the rough start to the day, I set up the laundry room, clean out the formal living room and start the process of turning it into an office, and bring in most of the boxes for what will be my actual media room. It's interesting to see how the Boomer generation (my parents) built their houses to have several rooms that only get minimal use on special occasions as if that meant middle class folks were as fancy as rich ones. I have no use for a living room full of uncomfortable 'receiving' furniture that only gets used during holidays or events. I also don't care to have a fancy looking 'living room' that isn't a dual use room for vegging out and watching Netflix with a tub of ice cream.

My mother would be horrified, I'm sure.

I'm converting the formal dining room into a mini-studio tomorrow—it has excellent light and enough space to allow me to set up my desk, easels, and storage cabinets with room to spare. I have no intention of throwing fancy dinner parties here, and the kitchen table and bar are good enough for me.

Niecy is sending her grandsons tomorrow to help move the outdated furniture to the truck and bring my more functional, comfortable pieces inside. They'll also help me arrange the upstairs once I get that far, and transport all the excess to the storage unit she arranged before I arrived.

Perhaps I can ask them who the hell my houseguests belong to. As if they can hear my thoughts, the cats yowl from the other room.

They're probably hungry—I sure as hell am.

Walking into the room, I see the terror twins batting a fluff ball back and forth and a smile rises to my lips. They're pretty cute when they act like real pets, I suppose. I put my hands on my hips and clear my throat. The cats turn, immediately sitting at attention with their eyes on me. That's kind of spooky, right? Aren't cats billed as the 'fuck you, human' of pets?

"Okay... uh..." I fumble for a moment, squatting to see if I can verify their genders before I nickname them for my convenience. Shit, I can't tell—my version of gender neutral it is. "Okay, Jekyll and Hyde, are you hungry?"

Jekyll stands on its hind paws, stretching up like a meerkat and bats at me. Is that a 'yes'? Hyde does the same, and I tilt my head. They tilt theirs in the exact same direction. I raise the hand opposite of the paw they're using; they change paws.

I keep saying it, but *what in the actual fuck*?

"Fine. Should we use DoorDash or go on a hunt in town?"

Jekyll yowls a response and bounds towards the door with Hyde in tow. Guess that means we're going out on the town.

I may be losing my ever-loving mind, folks.

○

Exiting the Impala, I snap my fingers and my uninvited guests follow at my heels as I stride towards the Atwater's grocery store. As far as I know, Percy's parents have resisted all attempts to be bought out by mega corporations that are dying to tap a money spigot like the wealthy folks in the Hollow. I'm sure a shiny new Whole Foods or Trader Joe's would love to be in place of Atwater General Store, but the folks in town don't like outsiders coming in to take over their old-world charm. I checked Google during my stint in traffic—there's a Wally World, a Whole Foods, and a Joe's within a short drive of town.

Yet on a random Monday evening, Atwater's is humming with activity. Looking at Jekyll and Hyde, I frown. The cats have refused to leave my presence since they appeared in my living room like a miniature hurricane. I don't know if Atwater's allows animals inside, and even if they do, it might be limited to service animals.

Before I can address my furry stalkers, Mayor Cornelia walks through the electronic doors, nearly slamming into me. I look up at her, taking in her youthful appearance and striking features.

"Jolene! Aldous mentioned he ran into you this morning. I

planned on contacting you later in the week once you were settled."

I smile, feeling nervous about meeting the woman that my parents called a 'juggernaut' of local politics as a fully grown adult. "That's very kind of you, ma'am. I'm doing well. I have lots to do, but I would love to connect with you once I'm moved in."

Her raven brow arches, and she looks down at the two servals standing on either side of me. "What's this? Souvenirs from your travels abroad? We don't have breed specific laws in town, Miss Whitley, but exotic animals will require licenses and collars if you are bringing them into town proper."

"You don't know who they belong to? These guys broke into my house earlier today and have become my stalkers. Servals are fairly expensive, and rare in the States, so I thought they must be pets that got out on someone."

Cornelia Sykes simply smiles at me mysteriously, her head shaking slowly. "No, I know all the exotic animals in town, and these two are not registered. The citizens of Whistler's Hollow know they would only need to ask for a license—I would never deny them a...partner... of choice."

My brows furrow in confusion at her wording, and I look down at the perfectly behaved, attentive cats at my feet. "Well, I'll check around before I decide. I appreciate your advice, ma'am."

Her raven tresses fly as she laughs. "Oh, Jolene! Stow that ma'am away for someone much more tightly wound than me. Call me Nelia. And..." she stops for a moment, as if weighing her words, "... you can ask young Wolfgang. As the town vet, he'd know if anyone had animals they were missing. However, I highly suspect that you, my dear, have been chosen."

Chosen? What the hell does that mean?

But I give the Mayor a polite nod and my typical pasted-on

'social smile' as I reply, "Thank you, ma—Nelia. I'll check with him and uh, think about what you've said."

"Don't worry, Jolene. No one will ask you to leave them outside. That's not how we do things here."

I blink, wondering how in the hell she knew exactly what I was thinking when we bumped into one another earlier. "Cool. And um, thanks again."

She winks at me, gives the cats a stare, and flutters off towards the parking lot with the air of a woman who knows that she is in charge of the world she lives in. I watch her get into the Rolls Phantom and speed off, chewing on my lip. What is it about the people in this town that make me feel like they have locked me in an escape room?

"MMrrrrrOOOW!"

"Oh, shit, Jekyll. You're right. We need to get some food before we all waste away," I reply absently. It doesn't occur to me I'm talking to them as if we're old friends and they speak English. I just knew he/she was trying to get my attention.

They trot behind me happily as I walk in, looking around to see if the store conjures up memories of when I was a child. Things should look familiar, but there's a... haze... ...around it all in my mind. I remember the registers—upgraded now to computer POS systems—and the produce section is sectioned differently because of the 'organic' craze but feels like it's the same. Running my hands over my face as I stand by a display of bananas, I close my eyes and try to imagine coming here with my parents.

I can't. And I know we came here all the time. It's just out of my grasp in a fuzzy space in my mind.

Hyde pushes his head into my palm, and I come out of the trance-like state I was in. I shake my head, heading for the fruits to pick up some snack food. I love junk food—I truly do—but I have to make certain that I eat enough fresh food. Not because of my weight, but because I get really slow and off when I don't consume the right amount of 'real' foods. I don't mean sick, loafy, or anything like a normal person. I mean, completely off-balance in a way the docs in Europe never did figure out.

"What should we get for dinner, guys? Pizza?" I murmur as I stuff berries and melon and assorted produce in my cart.

"*Mow!*" Jekyll answers.

Perhaps he doesn't want pizza.

Shit. I reach into my bag, pulling out my phone to Google 'serval cat diets' as I walk over to the beverage aisle to load up on my energy drinks. I'll need milk and ice cream for milkshakes as well, and some various flavoring to feed my habit. I'll get a pizza for me to heat up in the oven.

Chips! I would kill for Doritos. Whirling around, I head back to the aisle labelled snacks, and I run flat into *yet another* person.

I'm a one-woman wrecking ball today, I fucking swear.

"Easy there, Tíogair. No need to knock me into the bloody biscuits."

My face floods with color as I lift my head to apologize to the dude with the lilting accent. For the second time today, I'm completely speechless. I lick my lips, stalling as my eyes rove over the tattooed, leather wearing redhead with the mischievous glint in his eyes. He looks like a Weasley got run through a bad boy blender and he sounds like a hitman in an IRA movie.

What the *fuck* is in the water in this goddamned town?

"I..." Jekyll and Hyde save me by letting out low growls, their ears pinning back as their bodies tense on either side of me. Tearing my gaze away from the hot fucking leprechaun, I look down at them sternly. "It was my fault. Don't be dicks."

"Aye, lass. It's okay. Your wee caits don't scare me." His lips curl up as my stalkers take up their statue-esque seated poses and glare. "I'm glad you didn't knock the messages out of my arms, or I would have to get banjaxed at the sodding pub instead."

Luckily for me, I spent some time in Dublin on a project, so his pidgin English doesn't throw me for an even bigger loop. "Um, sorry about... almost knocking you down. I was... well, I wasn't watching where I was going because I have to get food for these guys. Seeing as we just met, I had to hit the web for answers. They didn't seem keen on pizza."

His chuckle makes me feel stupid, but he grins. "It's grand, Tíogair. I've got my stout, you've got your beasties, and we'll be on our way in no time."

I finally gather myself, giving him an annoyed look. I don't know what that stupid name means, but he's an arrogant little shit for thinking he can nickname me when he doesn't know my ACTUAL name. "Absolutely." I look down at the servals, my head tilted. "Let's go, Jekyll. Come on, Hyde. We have groceries to locate, and food to cook. No sense wasting any more time dilly dallying in the snack aisle."

With that, I flick my ponytail over my shoulder with the confidence of a Valley girl, turn on my heel, and head for the dairy section.

I'm going to need *two* milkshakes to get over that bullshit.

○

"And then he just kept *saying it*!" I grouse, propping my feet up on the coffee table. "Can you *believe* that?"

Jekyll and Hyde are perched on the couch they seem to have claimed as their own, eyes wide and ears perked up as they listen to me rant about Mr. Lucky Charms from the grocery store.

We ate well after I sorted out their diet—or the best info I could find online until I go see Hottie McBabyVet on Friday—

and now we're in the media room with British mysteries on in the background. I love a good mystery, and the greatest ones are on the BBC.

You can't convince me otherwise; don't even try.

"Mrrrrp?" Hyde questions, opening his mouth for another mini meatball.

"Exactly!" I lob the cooked meat into the air, and he leaps like a tiger to catch it in his mouth. Jekyll gives me an expectant look, and I load another meatball up. "What a douche canoe. No, not a douche canoe, a failboat. A failboat *full* of douche canoes. A goddamned *douche canoe navy*, that's it!"

Satisfied with my insult, I let the treat fly and this time, they both go for it. A minor scuffle ensues, and I wrinkle my nose. Greedy little shit, aren't you, Hyde? "Hyde! That's Jekyll's. Get back to your throne."

Amazingly, the little shit does just that.

The absolute bizarreness of everything that has happened since I set foot in this town is baffling. From the social media black hole to the hot guy parade to Hazel and now these guys, I can't figure out why I feel like I stepped into an episode of Twin Peaks. It never felt like this growing up. I noticed nothing different than a normal—albeit snooty—Southern town full of rich twats who think they own the universe. Why is it that every encounter I have here feels like the start of another mystery?

Shaking my head, I launch another meatball for Jekyll and then pick up the remote. I'm in the mood for Gracie Lou Freebush to take me to giggle town while I chow down on this granny apple-honey-mango milkshake I made. Thinking about all of the unusual people I've met is giving me a migraine.

As if the Universe is conspiring against me, the bloody doorbell rings.

Jekyll and Hyde leap into action, skidding across the oak floor to stop in front of it, their bodies tensed like a hound on a fox hunt. I've been on fox hunts, though it was reluctantly, and with the caveat that I wasn't killing a damned thing. The upper crust in England still participate in all sorts of ridiculous old traditions with business partners and when I contracted to the wealthy, I got roped into a *lot* of weird shit on client meets. The fetish club in Germany was one of the best ones, but that's because I spent most of the night analyzing the psychology behind the members' kinks in my head.

The doorbell peels again, and I huff.

Looks like I'm answering because the twin terrors are snarling at the door as if it's going to attack them on the spot.

"I'm coming! Hold your effing bits, I have to get decent!" I don't, but at least that declaration might stop the idiot at the door that has a fetish for button pushing.

I yank it open, my expression defiant as I cross my arms over my chest. When I see the person standing in front of me, I pale. The change in my posture makes Jekyll and Hyde snarl, and I reach down to touch each of their heads before they decide to tag team the giant on my porch. For one, given his size, I'm not certain they'd win, and secondly, knowing the power his family holds in this town, I worry he'd have my new amigos put down.

"Well, well, well. Looks like the Cotillion Catastrophe is all grown up."

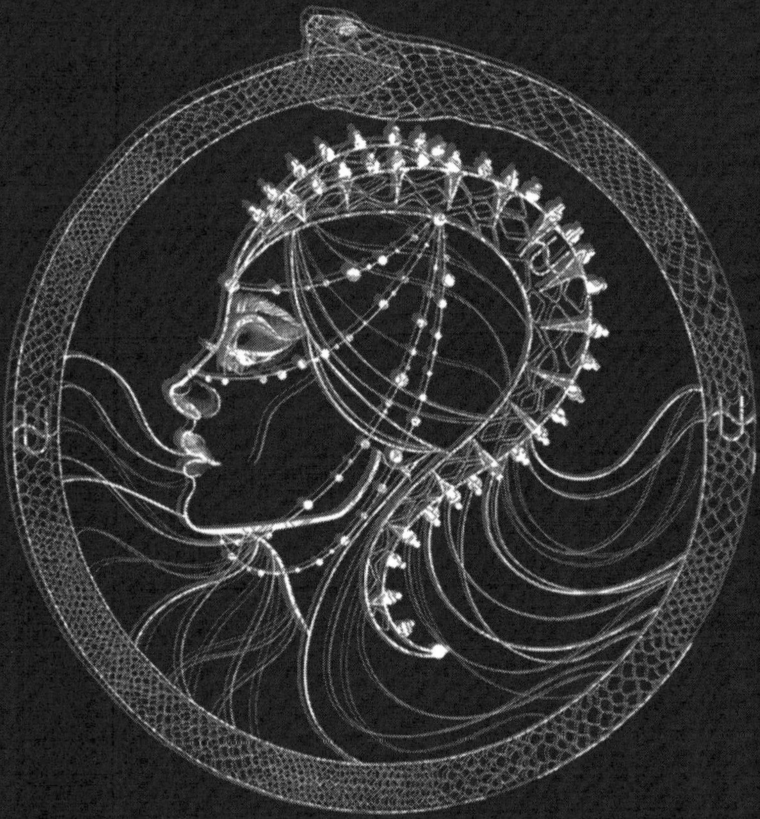

Brand New Me

Jolene

For a brief second, I consider spin kicking the smirk right off his goddamned face.

Instead, I re-cross my arms, giving him a look that drips with disdain. We are both too fucking old for this high school bully garbage. I've dined with the Pope, shopped with duchesses, and slept in castles. I'm not the paint covered, chunky nerd in braids anymore. I don't have to put up with his elitist claptrap.

"*Buena notte*, Edgar. What brings you to the slums this evening?"

Okay, that was petty. I'm not above being Petty Mayonnaise when the leader of the nasty rich kids from my high school nightmares shows up at my door at ten p.m. on a random Tuesday. His family is all about the Southern manners and genteel behavior, so where was my official notice of a visit? Must have gotten lost in the mail, right?

His infuriatingly handsome grin stretches, showing perfect pearly whites against his lush lips and dark stubble. A hand lifts to rake through his messy coal black hair, and I swear to seven levels of hell, it actually makes it look better. I watch him, keeping a bored look on my face as I study the expensive athletic gear, Supreme Chucks, and tanned skin he's sporting. He's clearly been keeping up his all-state, college QB physique over the years because every inch of him is on display in this get-up, and let's just say my libido has taken notice.

"Aw, Tilly, are you still holding a grudge about that stupid coming out party? It's been over a decade."

My brows furrow as I grit my jaw, hoping my facial expression remains impassive. He's right—my coming out cotillion was a Carrie-esque disaster of epic proportions, but there's a laundry list of other things I could hold a grudge over spanning all twelve years we were in school together. From ruined birthdays to school events and trips, society occasions, and even graduation, their group was always there torturing someone. Even if it wasn't me, I never condoned their behavior, and I won't let him excuse it now.

"Edgar, it's late. I've been working all day, and I'm relaxing before a week filled with similarly exhausting days unpacking. You can't seriously think I want to stand on my porch in my pajamas rehashing the past with you."

His eyes widen and he squints at me as if just noticing that he caught me unprepared to receive visitors. I immediately regret drawing attention to my appearance when he rakes his gaze from my toes up my bare legs to the tiny silk shorts with Monet's waterlilies on them. His smirk deepens as he hits my bare stomach, eyeing the glittering belly ring and intricate tattoo work that wraps around my left side, and follows the path to the lacy bralette. I try not to squirm—I refuse to give him the satisfaction—as he finally hits my face. He reaches out to tuck a strand of hair behind my ear, but my reflexes trump his. I smack his surprisingly elegant hand away from my face with a scowl.

"Ooh!" he says, shaking his hand and pouting. "Feisty. I like it."

With a narrowed gaze and a belly full of unresolved teenage rage, I crack my neck as I work to keep my legendary temper under control. "Edgar, I won't ask you again. You have five seconds to explain why the cock-gobbling fuck you're here or I'm slamming this door in your face."

I don't have to tell you which choice I'm hoping he makes. I'd love to crunch that perfect nose of his with my cherry wood door.

"Language, Tilly. It's not befitting a lady of your stature."

"Five... four..."

Raising his hands in surrender, the smoking hot asshole finally caves. "Okay, okay. Bobbi Jo had paperwork to send your way today, and like a true gentleman, I offered to deliver it in person."

Jekyll snarls at him. I arch a brow, looking down at the servals, noting their puffy tails. "Oh, Edgar. My friends here say that's a lie. Try again. Three... two..."

"Sweet baby Jesus, Tilly. Call off the little shits." He reaches into his back pocket and procures a manila folder, creased by his choice of storage space. "I'm only shading the truth a smidge. I was at the diner after you left today—listening to the buzz as usual—and Bobbi Jo came in. She said she was going to run these out to you, and I asked her to allow me. I was curious about the whispers, I'll admit."

I sigh, resigning myself to at least another fifteen minutes of this shit. I might as well do the whole 'guest in my home' Southern schtick now. He actually has a purpose for being here, though I suspect the timing and the true motivation for his drop-in is not the folder. "Okay, Edgar. Have a seat on the veranda and I'll look. I'm gonna go get a pen and my drink. Would you like a bourbon? I unpacked the bar yesterday."

His eyes light up like I've offered a meth addict a fix. "Single barrel, sugar? Neat."

Rolling my eyes into the back of my head, I turn on my heel and head into the house as he plants his gigantic frame in one of the two hand carved rocking chairs. My father made them before I graduated, and they've always been my favorites, so it's odd that he would pick those over the swing, rattan couches, or lounges. I flick the lamps on the lowest setting so I can see what I'm doing, but not high enough to bother my sensitive night vision.

When I'm satisfied that he's settled, I consider swapping my clothes to something less revealing. Hyde jumps up and places his paws on my ribs. The cats are almost as tall as I am when they stretch, and I wonder if they're full grown before shaking my head.

Christ, I'm so easily distracted.

"I suppose that's your way of telling me I look fine, buddy. I appreciate it. I didn't have the easiest time when I was younger, and I worked like a goddamned pack mule to get where I am today. He brings out all the insecurities from the past, I guess."

The cats tilt their heads at me, let out a resounding 'mow', and leap towards the kitchen. Even they think that's silly.

I pull two Baccarat rocks glasses out of the cabinet, smiling when I remember the friend who gave me this set while I was working on reputation repair for a chef in Italy. Studying my selection of single barrels, I select Blanton's, and pour three fingers in each glass. The training ingrained in my psyche immediately kicks in, and I find a tray to put the glasses on. I raid the fridge, making a small plate of cheese, fruit, and crackers, then add the bottle.

A Southern lady never makes her guests ask for anything, after all.

Putting the pen in my mouth, I lift the tray, balancing it like a pro, and make my way to the living room. I notice that Jekyll—the troublemaker—has grabbed the bag of meatballs in his mouth and is trotting along with a look of feline satisfaction. Hyde gives me a sheepish look, and I chuckle softly. I guess sets of twins are bound to have one good and one mischievous scamp—even in cats.

Edgar looks up as I pad onto the porch, his lips curling up. If he were as ugly on the outside as he is on the inside, this would be a lot fucking easier. He's always looked like a stinking superhero come to life, and that only made the grip his crowd had on our school tighter. Boys wanted to be him, and girls wanted to hump him, so all the little nasty deeds he and his cohorts committed were swept under the rug as pranks. The 'Nip Tucks'—as the rest of the girls called the pack of rich witches who ruled over us like third world despots in Prada—weren't much better. Their 'pranks' were vicious, and frequently escalated to injurious, but no one would acknowledge the damage they did.

My eyes fall on the folder on the table between the large chairs. I won't be a chickenshit like the teachers were in my day. Even if I'm only there part time, I won't allow whatever this generation's bitchy crew does to go unpunished. I'm not looking for revenge, but I won't turn a blind eye to kids' suffering, either.

"Why, look at you, Tilly! Your mama would be right proud," Edgar says, watching me carry my load without lifting a finger to help.

His mama would, too. Everyone in town knew that she treated her household staff as if she'd catch poor from them. I don't say that, though; I give him a tight smile. After all, he has no idea the turmoil I'm feeling over the past since returning, nor does he seem to be trying to be nasty. He assumes that I have a deeper connection to my parents than I feel. That's not his fault.

Sitting the tray on the table, I settle in the second rocking chair and wait for my furry guests to find perches on the closest lounge. I wasn't keen on their presence when they barged into my home, but I have to admit I'm fast growing used to their silent support. "Tell me about the paperwork."

He arches a brow, picking up his bourbon and taking a sip. His eyes widen in approval, and he gives me that shit-eating grin again. "Blanton's is an excellent choice, Tilly. The paperwork is just normal new hire stuff. Take your time and run it down to Bobbi Jo before Friday so Maryellen can get you set up in all the systems."

"Mrrrow," Hyde mutters.

Edgar chuckles and shakes his head. "Your companions don't like me very much, do they?"

I bite back a declaration of my agreement with them, and shrug. "I've always heard that cats are exceedingly particular about the company they keep. They must sense your more... mischievous side."

He throws back his head and laughs, a loud, belly deep sound that has him flashing the pearly whites of his perfect teeth and exposing his throat. His pulse jumps, and I frown, not sure why I noticed. His amusement flows over me like warm honey, and I can't help but smile along as I watch. When he catches his breath, his eyes catch mine, and something in them flashes, then disappears.

"Tilly, that's the best laugh I've had all week. I enjoy hearing a Southern girl try desperately to call me a twat in the politest language she can. I was right about your mama the first time—she'd be even prouder now. All you needed to add was 'bless your heart' and I'd have a fork in me."

I blink, my mouth opening and closing like a fish. So much for being subtle.

Before I can gather the tatters of my dignity, he rolls to his feet, yanks me out of the chair, and pulls me into his arms. I'm so shocked that a panicked squeak escapes me as he wraps my hair around his fist and tilts my head back. I swallow hard, tingles shooting down my spine when the hard planes of his body jut against the soft curves of mine.

"Teddy, what in the actual fu—"

The verboten moniker barely slips from my lips before he's kissing me. The rough scrape of his late-night stubble makes me sigh, and my arms wrap around him involuntarily. Ignoring the voice in my mind that's screaming 'what the holy fuck are you doing', I press against the hard planes of his broad chest and narrow hips. A low rumble echoes out of him, and his free hand slides down my side to my thigh, gripping it hard enough to leave a mark.

Our lips break for a second—almost long enough for me to put a stop to this madness—as he releases my hair. I open my mouth to protest, but he swoops in again, capturing my lips with a hunger that I can taste. He grabs my other thigh and lifts, wrapping my legs around his waist as he walks us towards the front door.

It occurs to me that my fierce protectors haven't so much as moved a whisker even though this brick wall of a guy is manhandling me. The feel of his teeth nipping at my lower lip brings me back to the asshat in question, and I raise my eyes to his. The aquamarine eyes I've admired since childhood are a dark blue green with flecks of jade as he looks at me as if he's waiting for something.

In what may prove to be the worst decision I've made since Thailand, I bury my fingers in his raven locks and yank his mouth back to mine. My body hums with excitement, pinpricks of electricity tingling over my skin like fireworks. Rocking my hips against his as he carries me one handed, I tug on the stylish waves at the nape of his neck. Our entire childhood feud flashes through my mind, but something lurking low in my gut demands that I listen to my aching pussy. It's been a very long time since I was physically intimate with someone, and I rarely know more than a first name and what they had to drink at the event I met them during.

I've always been a one and done girl, and I was careful to keep my selections away from the professional menu. You can't work for the Prime Minister of wherever if they find out you've fucked one of their relatives in the coat closet of an embassy. I never climb on the bull and ride with someone I know as well as I know this man.

"Stop thinking so hard, Tilly," he mumbles, nibbling my earlobe in a way that makes me shiver.

The nickname should put the flames in my belly out—it's a cruel reminder of the past—but something about the way he's saying it makes me clench in the best damned way. "Teddy... we..."

"Shh." His reply is almost hissed as he nips his way down my throat.

Hands squeeze my thighs as he carries me to the spare bedroom I camped out in until I deal with the master. I don't know how he found his way here, but he climbs onto the bed with me in hand, stretching over me like a goddamned panther. Heat floods through me, and I know without a doubt that he's going to fucking destroy me. "But..."

A huff escapes his lips, and he lifts off of me. I don't open my eyes for fear that I finally scared him away, and I'm not sure if that's really what I want.

Scratch that. It's definitely not what I want, and I might actually cry if I did.

The bed dips with the weight of a knee in the mattress, and I almost whimper in relief. Soft silk slides over my torso, making the plethora of bare skin goose-pimple as it travels to my face. His lips touch my ear again, his tone low and husky. "Brattiness has consequences, Tilly."

I have no idea what he plans to do with one of my silk scarves, but in for a penny, right? "I'm sure I have no idea what you mean, Teddy."

The nickname makes him growl, and my clit throbs in response. "When I say 'shhhh', I mean it, sugar."

The scarf whispers over the marks he left on my neck until it reaches my lips, and I realize he plans to keep my big, fat mouth from ruining this. He allows me to refuse, and when I don't, he slips the fabric between my lips. His long fingers tie the material in a loose knot at the back of my head, but he gives me room to wiggle it loose if I choose. My nipples harden at the thought of those hands on me in other places, but since I'm effectively gagged, I rely on tactile sensation to make my point.

Edgar Olivier Boone III has a domination fetish, and I'm on board. He's also moving far too slowly for my taste now.

I grab his hips and yank him closer, arching up to grind my core against him. A chuckle tickles my collarbone, followed by a firm nip, and I wriggle under him again, trying to force him to move at my speed. His hands slide from my shoulders to my thighs, and he yanks them apart to settle his hips between mine. The feeling of victory swells in my chest, but he simply continues biting and leaving marks across my collarbones.

"Sugar, I can promise you that there isn't a thing in the entire universe that's gonna rush this. If I need to take more drastic measures to keep you still, I'll do so." A gentle tug on my nipple piercing and the wetness of his mouth dampening the fabric of my bralette punctuates his last remark.

I sure as fuck didn't plan on this when I dressed for lounging in my house with a milkshake, but I'll be damned if my legendarily fickle luck hasn't struck again. A sharp rap on my hipbone brings me out of my thoughts, and I make a sound as the sting travels straight to my eager vagina.

"Get out of your head, Tilly. I want you present and accounted for, especially if that means you'll give me more of that bratty attitude," Edgar orders as he peels my top off and tosses it like it didn't cost an arm and a leg.

I'd answer if I could speak, but since I can't, I do the next best thing: I tug on his hair hard, pulling it in my best effort to give him the impertinence he asked for. I want him to fuck me, and I want it now, and if he doesn't, I'm going to leap off this bed and find something to help my damn self.

As if he heard my thoughts, the bully from my youth dives in and takes a nipple in his mouth at the same time as his hand snakes right up the leg of my shorts. His elegant fingers strum over my mound, a low growl vibrating around my ring when he discovers that I'm commando under the waterlily shorts. His fingertips slide along my slit, spreading the embarrassing flood of wetness there, and I close my eyes. The shudder that rocks my frame is not subtle, and he lifts his head, blowing cool air on the stiff peak he was suckling.

His voice is a whisper against my stomach as he moves down my body, trailing kisses and nibbles and sharp bites like he's tasting me. He yanks the shorts off quickly, his voice low and snarling. "Tilly, I'm going to make you scream so loud the neighbors will wonder if someone murdered you. And when I'm done with that, I'm going to break this motherfucking bed, so you have to buy a new one—preferably larger."

The last addition makes me snort, and his lips curve into a smile against my skin. He doesn't know that I don't intend to do this ever again, especially since we'll be working together, but if it makes him feel like he's in charge, he can pretend to demand things.

Then his mouth touches me and every fucking thing I've learned in my damn life falls out of my head. His lips graze the bare skin lightly, tracing around the shape of my sex slowly. The tip of his tongue follows the same path, and I want to scream in edged frustration, but I won't give him the satisfaction. I dig my nails into the ugly ass comforter and physically will myself not to move or make a sound.

Mostly because I'm afraid if I let one slip, I'm going to turn into the banshee he promised, and I'll *never* live that shit down.

"I said, get out of your head, Tilly," he murmurs, before flicking his tongue over my clit so quickly that I almost think I imagined it.

The shocks flying up my frame disagree, and I bite back another groan. I am *so* incredibly *fucked* and I don't mean by that monster I felt rubbing against me earlier—at least, not yet.

I lift my head, opening my eyes to look down at him lounging between my thighs as he waits for me to do as instructed. His lips glisten with my juices, and his fingers are tapping the apex of my pussy in a light rhythm that's making my thighs shake. If I had use of my mouth, I'd snark about performance anxiety, but I tuck my chin, bite the scarf in my mouth, and smile invitingly.

His eyes widen and he tilts his head for a brief second before throwing my legs over his shoulders and fucking devouring me. Lips, teeth, and tongue go wild on my slick heat, and my legs fold around him so tightly that I worry I might actually suffocate him. The sound he makes when he thrusts two fingers inside of me and bites my clit is like nothing I've ever heard before. There's a slight pinch and before I know it, my mind is flying like I'm on molly.

Blinking, I arch my back and let out the longest, loudest moan I've ever heard come of out of my body as spasms make my limbs jerk and twitch. The orgasm feels like it's wringing every drop of energy from my body, and my fingers tear into the comforter for purchase. Something soft and feathery coasts over my thighs, tickling the sensitive skin and making me writhe more.

My heart thuds, my blood crashes through my veins like I'm going to explode, and my lungs can't seem to find enough air to fill them. His skin is a furnace against mine, and I can't for the life of me figure out how he got naked without me noticing.

As I tremble, Edgar slithers his way up my body, his eyes shining brilliantly as he removes the makeshift gag and ducks his head to kiss me. Our mouths battle and before I can recover from the intensity of my climax, his hips jerk and he's inside of me. The stretching of my muscles to accommodate him burns, fanning the liquid lava in my veins, and something deep in my belly stirs.

I lift my arms, wrapping them around him, and digging my nails into his hips hard. He must like it, because a snarl followed by a soft sound echoes out of him. When he moves, I try to find my bearings, but my mind is scattered and euphoric as the sensations sizzle over my skin. There's no coming back from this experience, and I'm not a girl who has lacked for sexual partners when I chose to find them.

Edgar Olivier Boone III is *ruining* me, and I can't find a single fiber of my being that seems to care.

"Son of a *bitch*," he whispers as he lifts his head to allow us both to catch our breath, his hips still pounding against mine.

The sheer force of our coupling may actually break the goddamned bed as he promised, and the spark in my belly that stirred grows. I can feel warmth seeping out of me like tendrils of energy licking over my skin to get to him. When it reaches him, his head jerks up from my neck, and his eyes flash from aquamarine to a deep black and back again. His chest rumbles and his hips speed up, moving impossibly fast with mine, driving me into the mattress like a prowling beast.

The moment the second orgasm hits me, I know it triggered

his because an unearthly roar escapes his lips, and he throws his head back as our bodies tense. A cool wind comes out of nowhere, breezing over us in a gentle touch, and a low whisper of sound accompanies it. Holding onto him tightly, I ride out our pleasure as our limbs stutter and fall to the bed.

"*Drugar.*"

That's the last thing I hear before everything goes dark.

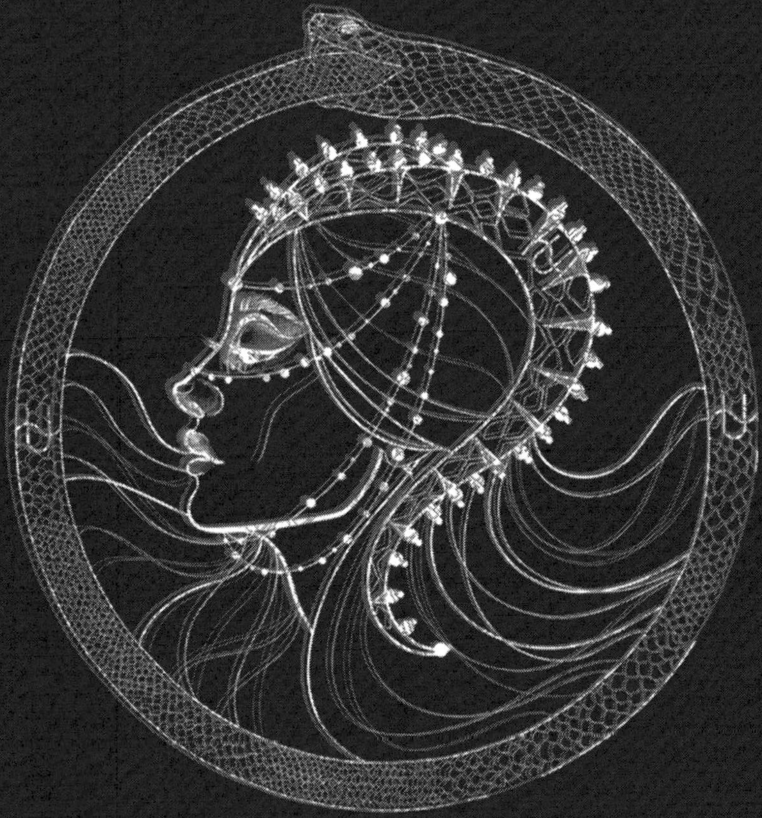

Small Town Girl

Jolene

Did anyone get the plate on that fucking semi?

My eyes fight me as I pry them open through sheer force of will. The light pouring into the guest room is so bright that it makes me want to hurl, and I know I didn't drink more than a glass of bourbon with...

Holy goddamned frog balls—Edgar.

I. Fucked. Edgar. Olivier. Boone. III. Last. Night.

If I hadn't been there, I wouldn't believe me, either. Speaking of which, I look around to find that I'm nestled on the couch—not in the bedroom—and there's a suspicious *absence* of dude I banged anywhere to be seen. Of bloody course he took off like his ass was on fire. I've known the douche my entire life; I should have seen this coming—typical dude bro, skating the second he hits it.

Closing my eyes, I think back to what I can sort out in my hazy brain, and frown. I mean... it was pretty spectacular. I'm not gonna tell him—obviously—but that was easily top five material for my mental spank bank. It's odd that he fucked off without even leaving a note.

"*Mow!*" Jekyll yells from the kitchen.

That's true. I haven't left the living room to see if there are any notes. Or any lurking porn star, ex-school bullies in workout clothes, either.

I slide my legs off the couch and move to sit up. Oh, Jaysus, Mary and the Holy Orgasm—as Saoirse would say—I think my entire body is broken. Getting to my feet and wobbling without collapsing, I slowly make my way to the kitchen, grumbling about the light, the aches, and stupid hot guys I'll have to face at work.

Why, oh why, did I break one of my cardinal rules?

I grope until I find a sugary, flavored coffee pod, a mug, and a scrap of dignity. Once it brews, I shuffle to the fridge and pull out a baggie full of chopped meats for the cats, arranging them on a plate. They hop onto the high counter, and I can't find it in me to care. I don't want to attempt bending over yet.

"Just where the hell were you two when I was making bad fucking decisions?" I ask.

Hyde lifts his head from the plate, blinks once, and ducks down like he's ashamed. Jekyll simply yells with his mouth full, and I grunt.

Great—cat spittle. That seals the deal on this disaster or a morning.

○

Making my way down the stairs carefully, I glare at the front door as if it's offended me. Perhaps it has, given that it's what Edgar stood in front of last night. My companions follow on either side, observing me. They didn't flinch when I threw my mug at the wall after discovering the broken bed in the guest room, and they just watched while I got dressed, cursing every single bruise and mark on my pale skin.

This is *definitely* worse than Thailand.

It took almost an hour to clean up the bedroom mess, find clothes, shower, and make myself look presentable. I have to go into town to get another set of paperwork from the school—like hell I'm turning in Edgar's rumpled bullshit—and although I want to avoid downtown like the plague, I now need to browse the shops for furniture.

And possibly a bag for my stupid head so I can hide my embarrassment when my poor judgement inevitably gets around.

As much as I hate to admit it, the only proper furniture and belongings I kept in my apartment in Richmond either involved my media room, my desk, and my studio equipment. I never intended to settle in there, and my singular focus on getting ready for my F.B.I. career kept me from doing normal human stuff like that. My mattress and box springs were on the floor. I kept my clothes in plastic totes and in the closet, and I spent zero time on making it look like a home.

Even when I finish unloading the small truck and send away the stuff that belonged to my parents, I won't have much in the way of décor. That might not matter in other places, but in Whistler's Hollow, it will start gums flapping. I don't need people whispering about my lack of genteel graces; I need them to trust me so I can figure out how to fix whatever this godforsaken place did to my background check.

The sooner I do that, the sooner I can get on with my actual life.

I'm not naïve enough to believe that I'll understand it overnight. Hell, it might even take years. I have to settle in, worm my way past their aristocratic defenses, and ferret out what I need. It's like a long-term undercover mission, and the deeper under I go, the more likely I'll be to gather the intel.

For today, that means furniture and clothing shopping. IKEA and Amazon won't cut it in the Hollow.

With that gem of knowledge, I walk into the kitchen and grab my bag. Jekyll and Hyde look up at me curiously, and I sigh. "We're going shopping, guys. Behave so I don't have to explain to Mayor Cornelia why you mauled some idiotic rich dude, please? I don't have the spoons to deal with any more drama."

They yowl, and I take that as agreement. The keys jingle in my hand as we walk to the garage, gun the engine on the Impala, and head for viper's nest.

○

Pulling into a spot on the lot near Town Hall, I look across the dash to see Jekyll and Hyde slinking back into the car. They rode shotgun with their heads out the window like two hyenas belonging to a harlequin, and it made me smile for the first time all day.

"Well, my dudes, are we ready to wreck some havoc?"

"*Mrrrrrow!*"

I chuckle at their enthusiasm, climbing out of the low-slung car carefully. I ache from head to toe, and despite the concessions I made when choosing an outfit, I wince when I rise to my full height. Standing still, I pretend to adjust my custom aviators while the screaming pull of my muscles relaxes. I'm sure anyone who's seen me more than once in this town has wondered why I always stop after I exit my car—it probably looks like a redheaded cop in a police procedural. There's a reason every time, and most of the fiddling with my glasses has to do with my incredibly light sensitive eyes. They've always been an issue, and no one could ever explain why.

Thus, special spy glasses as payment for a discreet favor from the friend from 6.

Jekyll and Hyde leap across the seat, landing next to me gracefully, and I shut the door. My bag bumps against my finger-marked hip as I slowly stride towards the middle of Main Street. Gritting my teeth against the sting, I cross the street, making a beeline for Grant Home Furnishings first. The furniture part of this excursion will take the least time and cause me the least amount of pain.

My phone rings, the sound of Holst's *Jupiter* echoing out of my bag. I move to lean against the wall of the shoe store while I dig it out. Jekyll and Hyde move in front of me, their large eyes squinting into the light as they watch the passersby while I bobble my phone around. Note to self: Amazon cat eye some things because they look pained.

"This is Whitley," I answer.

"Well, I'll be wired to the moon! It's about bloody time I heard from you."

Letting out a breath of relief, I smile despite the shittiness of my morning. A nice long chat with Saoirse is exactly what the doctor ordered. I frown as my closest friend describes every little thing that's happened since we spoke two weeks ago. We don't get to talk as often as I'd like—my quest for F.B.I. acceptance and her high-profile career as personal seamstress to the wealthy often keep us from doing more than texting or swapping memes on social media.

"I've missed you, Seer. Where have you been?" Her tinkling laughter makes me smile, and I listen to her describe her antics at a party for a well-known movie star at Cannes. I met Saoirse when I was on assignment with a CEO's daughter in Dublin, and we hit it off immediately. Hearing her voice makes me feel a little less like an outsider looking in, and I decide to forego the furniture for a little while longer while we chat. "Well, what did the Sultan's son do when you dumped a bowl of fondue in his lap?"

"He said, 'you'll pay for that, peasant' and I said, will I yea? Then the little shit threw a bloody fit and the entire party went minus craic in a flash. If you'd been there, you would have been up to 90, and we would have both ended up in jail again, Peanut."

My nose wrinkles. Seer will *never* let me forget Thailand and when she hears what a monumental fuck up my move here has been, she'll laugh until she busts a seam in whatever monstrosity she's sewn herself into today. "Seer, you know I hate when you call me Peanut. Plus, you forgot the cardinal rule—if his net worth could buy my hometown's GDP, we stay *away*."

"Y'can't invoke the 'if the family has sheikhs, the thighs don't quake' rule. I was off my head on ouzo, and my supposed date disappeared with some underwear model—and I don't mean a lass."

I cover my mouth with my hand, snickering. Saoirse has the rottenest taste in men I've ever seen. "Seer, you can't toss all the rules in the bin just because I'm here and you got hammered. The rules are final—you know that."

"*Mow!*" Hyde proclaims loudly.

"What the feck is *that*?"

I sigh, looking around to see why he yelled. Squinting, I catch sight of the reason for his distress. When I see the man strolling towards the diner, I nearly drop my phone. Oh, I do *not* want to face Edgar the escape artist before I even have my coffee. "Seer, I gotta go. There's... uh, an issue. Talk soon!"

Clicking the phone off before she can answer, I jerk my head at the cats and scurry as quickly as I can towards my original destination. I push the door open, cringing at the loud jingling bell as our motley trio enters. Ducking around a corner, I peek out the window, watching the broad shoulders of the jackass who left me to deal with our mess alone stride down the opposite side of the street.

If I didn't know better, I'd think I saw him frown as he passes the Grant's even though I know he can't see me.

"Excuse me. I'm Zelda Amelie Grant, and I'd love to assist you if you need it."

The voice catches me off guard, and I suck in a breath. "Oh, shit. Um...it's okay, Mrs. Grant. I can... I can look around first."

Her sharp gaze looks at me as if she's going to flay my soul from my body. "Jolene Whitley," she spits. Her tone is now disapproving, and the lines around her mouth are deeper. "What in the name of all that's holy are *you* doing in my store?"

I blink in confusion. Her son, Dylan Marlowe Grant, married one of my high school tormentors, but he was a couple of years older than us. I have no idea why she'd react like this. Sherilynn never saw me as more than a speck of dirt on her Pradas, so I can't imagine she's relayed anything that would cause a random town maven to act like I just pissed on her carpet. "Uh... I'm looking for...furniture?"

Sniffing, Zelda looks me up and down, judging my platform Chucks, leggings, and zip up yoga sweater. "I'm certain that you won't find anything here to suit your tastes."

Did this bitch just tell me I'm too skanky to shop in her store?

Jekyll and Hyde rear back, their tails puffing as they snarl at her. Zelda lets out a squeak of fear, and I tilt my head at her. My instincts say that I can't attack this old lady, but something inside of me wants to teach her a lesson. I've never felt the need to make someone submit so keenly as I do right this second.

A piercing whistle echoes off the walls, and my hands unclench from fists to cover my ears. Jekyll and Hyde immediately drop to the floor, their heads going into their paws. I'm sure with their animal hearings and large ears, they're suffering even more than I am. The sound stops, and I turn to look at the source of the sound.

Standing in the doorway to the back of the store is yet another ass-clenchingly hot dude. He pulls his fingers from his plump lips, grinning as he stands there—shirtless, I might add—and looks at the commotion. "What in the seventh circle of Hades is going on? Zelda, you asked me to help evict the family of redbirds from your rafters, not calm wild kitties."

The harpy in front of me blushes beet red, her bony hand fluttering at her collarbone. "Presley Hamilton! You are not dressed for receiving company—even if it is unwelcome visitors."

My glare narrows and I look at the bitch who just insulted me a *second* time in two minutes while I'm trying to buy shit from her damned store. Hyde growls this time, and I touch his head, hoping he knows that means to chill. "I don't know, Z. Looks like he's dressed to be receiving something, but I doubt it's what you'd like him to."

His rich laugh skates over my skin as the Botoxed bat huffs loudly. She's only two decades older than me, but I can promise you she was on the prowl like some fucked version of a cougar from TV. Kim Cattrall she ain't, but that's never stopped a washed-up Southern belle in the past.

"I'm Jolene Whitley. I moved back here a day or so ago. I needed some furniture to replace the stuff at my folks', but..." I glance around, purposefully curling my lips in dissatisfaction. "... I can see that this is a little old school for my taste. I'll let you get back to your bird removal, Mr. Hamilton."

Sexy bird man arches a brow, his lips twitching at my word choice. "I apologize for my appearance, Jolene. Miss Zelda's crawl space is a bit musty."

"I'll bet it is," I mutter under my breath. Making a clicking sound, I look at Jekyll. "Are you ready to go, boys? I think we'll need to look at more contemporary designs online. I don't want to live in a museum."

Zelda makes an affronted sound and I smile internally. That'll teach her to *Pretty Woman* me. I shoot the hot dude a wink, pretending to stroll out so he doesn't notice my shuffling walk of shame. I'm out the door when I hear him call after me.

"Oh, and Jolene? It's Dr. Hamilton."

I keep waking until I'm out the door, carrying my yet again shredded dignity in hand as I curse under my breath.

Of fucking course it is.

○

After that clusterfuck, I decide that I'm not going to attempt clothes shopping until I acquire another cup of coffee. It's a risk—the diner is a favorite spot of those from Town Hall and the courthouse, so I could conceivably run into Mr. Dine and Dash—but my caffeine addiction wins against my irritation.

Walking down the street, I look at the shops with a keen eye, muddling out the provenance since they will essentially be my neighbors. Grant Home Furnishings is at the far end of Main Street, closer to the schools and Atwater's. Next, the professional offices like Hamilton Clinic, Fletcher Veterinary, and the *Hollow Hollar* fill wide spaces. I peek into the window of the paper, unsure who might run it now. My eyes fall on the unmistakable face of Amy Matilda Behle at a desk in the back and I hot foot it away quickly. That's not a bridge I want to cross this soon, either. Looking across the street, I see Derby Pies (the pizza joint), Tame Your Mane (the salon), and Bound Together (the bookstore).

I'm not sure why all the people here feel like their niche stores need corny names, but I can promise you, I'm sticking with

Whitley Gallery. I don't need to brand myself a small-town rube, thank you very much.

Passing the Happy Happy Toy Toy, the Star-Spangled Bank, Close Encounters of the Baked Kind, Bottles 'N Cans—which I shit you not—has an image of clapping hands in the logo. I wonder if they made weed legal in this state. I didn't pay attention while I was busy staying as far away from the Hollow as I could, but it would sure as hell explain the naming scheme here.

I stop blinking as I hit the florist.

There's no bloody way.

I *have* to have breathed in varnish at that stupid old crone's store.

The fucking florist's shop is named Wild Astor Plants—with the first letters twice the size of the rest of the words. There is *no way* that's a design error.

A chuckle sounds behind me, and I'm too stunned to even react.

"Yeah, I told Doyle that updating all these store names to trendy stuff isn't going to make us go viral or anything, but he never listens."

Arching a brow, I turn, and my jaw drops. Is the Universe actively trying to make me lose my shit?

The dude standing behind me is another fucking supermodel. He's the picture of a Latin lover with his dark hair and olive skin, and as if that wasn't enough, he has the most unique eyes I've ever seen. They're deep black, ringed with brilliant white and I wonder if that's some genetic thing or if he's just wearing SFX contacts. The effect is shiver worthy, and I blink at him like an idiot as I stare into them.

"Um, well. I... mean..."

New hot guy laughs and tilts his head. "It's a genetic thing. The eyes, I mean. I know it's shocking at first..."

My face heats and I know I must be beet red. "I'm sorry. I didn't mean to stare. It's just..."

"No worries. I'm used to it."

I try to regain some composure as I turn back to the storefront. "Do the owners have any idea what he's gotten them into?"

"No," he rumbles. "They haven't a clue. This town is very sheltered from the outside world, and well, Doyle has a mischievous streak a mile wide. I think it amuses him that they don't get the jokes."

Frowning, I waffle over whether that's funny—because a lot of these people have enormous sticks up their asses—or mean.

"It's funny, trust me. At least, it is until they figure it out, and then it'll be a headache for Nelia."

"How did you—never mind." I shake my head, unwilling to ask if I got caught thinking out loud again. I already look like an idiot. "Well, good luck to him when it lands on her desk. She's not one to take excuses. At least, she never was when I was growing up."

Gorgeous eye guy tilts his head and gives me a small smile. "You're the girl who just moved back, right? The one teaching art and opening a gallery?"

I nod, gesturing in the direction of the space that will hold the gallery. "That's me. I'm Jolene Whitley. And you are....?"

"Hugo. I teach history," he says, suddenly looking off into space as if he heard something.

Shit. Am I that boring? Did pretty eyes just space out before I could even finish introducing myself? That's it. I'm zero for five in the smoking hot dude department. Even the Bengals wouldn't draft me and that's saying something.

"Jolene, I apologize for my rudeness, but I must hurry. Please come see me once you get settled and I'll fill you in on the staff." He gives me a smile, acting like he didn't just pluck one of my biggest worries out of thin air, and hurries down the street towards Atwater's.

I watch him go, speechless for the ten millionth time since I arrived in my hometown.

"Mow!"

Looking down, I frown at the cats at my feet. "Where the hell did you guys go? I made an idiot of myself again, and you Houdini'd out, so you couldn't save me," I gripe. They just give me big eyes for a moment, then turn tail towards the diner. Grumbling under my breath, I give in, following them down the street with a deep-seated plea to the universe that I don't encounter anyone else that wants to socialize.

I'm peopled out for the day and it's only 10 am.

○

When I enter the diner, I'm thrilled to find it mostly empty. The Town Hall crowd hasn't started filtering in for lunch, and the breakfast people are gone. There are a few old timers in booths towards the back, but the noise level is low, and my chances of being accosted seem much the same.

"Miss Jolene!" Hazel calls, hoofing it from the other end of the counter to meet me. "You're back. And you've found friends, I see."

I look at Jekyll and Hyde, who promptly leap onto counter stools as if presenting themselves at a cat show. "I did. Have you seen them before? They sort of showed up two nights ago and refuse to leave."

Hazel's smile widens and she shakes her head. "No, I haven't. You seem to have been chosen." Bustling away for a moment, she returns with two small plates with pieces of lunchmeat on them, sitting one in front of each cat. "Such lovely gentleman deserve a treat, I think. What can I get for you, Jolene?"

"Just a to-go cup with the largest amount of cream, sugar, and vanilla syrup you can fit in it. I've had an interesting morning, and I have a few more things to pick up before I head home to tackle the upstairs of the house."

"Mmmm," she says, arching a brow. "People giving you trouble? Send them to Hazel and I'll set them straight."

Chuckling softly, I shake my head. "No need, Hazel. Over the years, I've gotten quite skilled at taking care of myself. I'm not the little girl who lived here years ago. But I appreciate the offer."

She harumphs, walking over to the cappuccino machine when it beeps. I watch her carefully pour the coffee, add a few things in unmarked bottles, mix, and then dollop foam on the top. "If you say so. Just remember that I'm here if you change your mind. Where are you headed next?"

I take a sip of the drink she hands me, and my eyes almost roll back into my head. Whatever this is, it's heaven on Earth. I know better than to ask baristas, bartenders, and cooks for their secrets, so I smile. "I have to go down to *Dress Me Up Buttercup* to buy some clothes that are a little more...here...for when I teach."

A booming laugh echoes off the walls, and Hazel looks over at my companions. "You two keep her calm in there. Fidelia Violet Cantwell isn't the worst of the ladies in this town, but she isn't the best, either. And if her brother is around, avoid him like the plague. That little twit is FAR too big for his britches."

"Hazel!" I admonish, looking around to make sure prying eyes or nosy ears aren't going to spread rumors that I trashed founding families in public. "I'm sure everyone has grown up since I left."

"You'd be one hundred percent wrong, Jolene. None of them have, and it worries me for a lot of reasons. Since the Hostile

Takeover, things should be moving in the right direction, and they don't seem to be."

My brow arches. 'The Hostile Takeover'? What in the hell is that?

"Well, even so, I want you to be careful. I'm not someone the Council will take notice of, even if I am disrespecting our elite townsfolk. You, however, need to toe the line when dealing with them. The big families are protected, and I don't want to see you end up like…"

Her words trail off, and I lean in, hoping she lets a few more clues slip. My gut instinct is that Hazel knows something that could start me on the path to solving my mystery, but if I push too hard, she'll shut down. "Like whom, Hazel?"

"No," she murmurs. "It's not time yet." Frowning, she walks over and picks up the empty plates in front of my boys, lumbering to the back with them.

Damnit. I almost got real intel. It was so close I could taste it. If only Hazel hadn't trailed off, I would have gotten a name to start researching. I wait for a few moments, and when it's clear that Hazel isn't coming back out, I gather my bag and coffee, disappointment etched across my features.

My fickle luck strikes again.

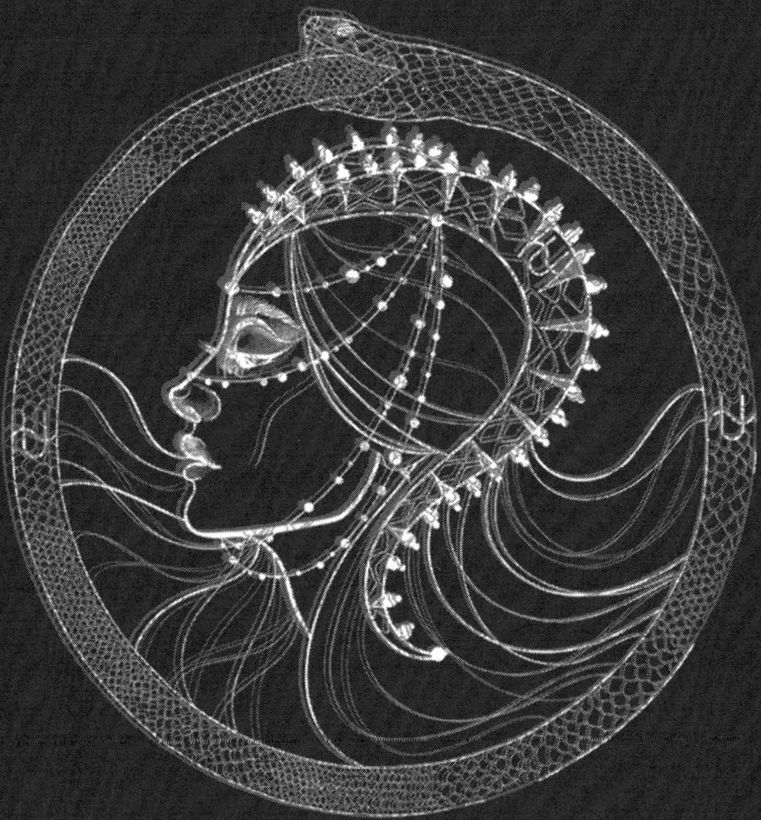

Home (Again)

Jolene

"Oh, come on!" I growl in frustration. The pieces of the broken bed are heavy as shit because my parents had a love affair with furniture built to withstand an earthquake. I thought I could at least get them into the hallway before Gene and Niecy's grandkids show up.

I piled the bags and boxes containing my new clothes on the lounge, and though my visit with Fidelia was definitely not one I look to repeat, it wasn't the worst interaction I've had. I finished my shopping, came home, and worked on the downstairs boxes until it was done.

Unfortunately, that meant bunking on the couch again, and since I'm not a twenty-year-old anymore, it needs to be the last time. Or at least, the last time until I get my furniture inside. The remnants of my folks' décor are all uncomfortable yet highly presentable for guests. The sparse items I bought in Richmond are designed for comfort and function, not snotty tea parties, so getting those unloaded is another priority for the day.

My dreams were filled with weird symbols and events—so

much so that I remembered every second of them when I woke up. Usually, I get fragments, but not much else.

Everything here is off-kilter, and it's making me batty.

I give the huge chunk of bed frame another shove, using my entire body to slide it through the doorframe. "*Finally*."

I drop to the floor, panting as I fumble for my water bottle. There are piles of boxes in every room of the upstairs, each labelled with its contents. I know that I'll have to have Niecy's boys clear the broken bed first, and then every single piece of furniture from that master before I can unpack. I don't feel comfortable in my parents' room, and I can't live in the smaller guest room I'm in now.

Ironically, this was my bedroom growing up, but once I was off to college, my folks re-did it. It stung a little that they didn't even wait a full year after I left to get rid of my room, but I shrugged it off like I did every eccentricity my folks had. I'm sure they packed away my stuff in the basement, but that's a project for another day.

I need to finish the upstairs today, because tomorrow I have the visit with Hottie McBabyVet at the farm and I have to take my paperwork in to Bobbi Jo. They will complete the deliveries to the studio by Saturday, and I have to head there to set up the basics and the classroom space. Monday is the first day of teacher orientation at WHFS.

Time is moving so quickly, and I'm not remotely ready.

○

Niecy's grandkids are adorable, lanky teenagers with saucy wits—just like their grandmother. They loaded up the broken pieces with raised eyebrows, but their ingrained Southern manners kept them from asking what happened. I was grateful for that given that I didn't want to share the NC-17 story of my shame with anyone—much less a bunch of teenagers and a man I think of like a grandfather.

Gene directed them while they carried out every scrap of furniture in my parents' bedroom, leaving piles of knickknacks, clothes, and other items around the perimeter for me to sort into categories. The storage facility is two towns over, so they'll be gone long enough for me to unbox some of my own things and use the boxes to designate what's going to storage, what is getting donated, and what is trash. Gene wisely suggested that I make a trash pile that they will use the truck to take to the dump rather than have it sit around waiting for the garbage day I missed on Monday.

You'd think after years of gallivanting around Europe on my own, I'd be good at this adult shit, but I'm fast realizing that being a nomad meant I learned absolutely zero about what normal people do day to day. I guess living like a college/grad student for half a decade didn't help, either. I'm lucky I have Gene and the others to help integrate me into society or I'd be in real trouble.

Who worries about this kind of stuff when they might immigrate to another country in a few weeks? Not me, that's for sure.

I plop down in front of a pile of books, papers, and miscellaneous junk that my parents kept in their drawers in the master. I'm not ready to look at clothing yet—it feels so personal, and I have such conflicted feelings about them right now.

After stacking a bunch of correspondence in a plastic bin that held shoes, I turn my attention to an ornately carved boxed that sat on my mom's vanity for as long as I can remember. The detail work is exquisite, and I wonder if it was a gift or something they had made. Squinting, I try to recall if I ever saw my mom open it, and though my memory is hazy, I can't find a single memory of this box being anything but locked and displayed on the table.

Running my fingers over the painted teak, ivory, silver, and mother-of-pearl insets, I wrinkle my nose. The design on the top looks very familiar, but I can't place it. I know that I've seen it before—in fact; I believe I've seen it many times. But it's not the logo of an artisan or company or anything like that. No, this is something that I've seen in smoky rooms and dark meetings. The harder I try to figure it out, the more elusive it becomes in my mind.

Damnit. I have an eidetic memory about everything in the Universe except my ruddy past. I hate it.

I turn the box around in my hands, searching for clasp or keyhole, but there isn't one. I'm certain there's something special inside, but I'll be fucked if I know what it is. It's not making a sound when I shake it, but deep in my gut I know it contains important stuff. Growling, I sit the puzzle box aside, vowing to work on it more this evening when I've earned time to be irritated. For now, I have a shit ton of stuff to sort before Gene and the boys get back for another load.

My parents weren't wealthy like the elite families, but I knew we weren't average middle class, either. Investigating the jewelry boxes, rolls, and containers only confirms my suspicions, because my mother has pieces I know are worth a pretty penny. Taped to the bottom of one box is a note that says 'Box 1989, 687626767, 565363, 492743#75, Tom/Card/PiggyWeeWee/Bell/FuckYou' in my mom's looping handwriting.

What. In. The. Hell.

Eloise Clara Whitley *never* cursed. I never in my entire life span heard my mom utter anything worse than taking the Lord's name in vain, even if she injured herself.

It feels like a stone has settled in my gut. I'm certain this won't be the first odd thing I find in my parent's belongings, and that notion makes me slightly ill. The mystery that brought me back to

Whistler's Hollow may be connected to the disconnect between what I can remember about life here and all the unusual shit I'm running into.

That does not bode well.

My experience is that if people hold secrets over decades, they won't let go of them easily. In fact, the longer a secret remains buried, the less likely is it to be discovered. Human nature is inclined to preen under the attention of having knowledge others don't, and the fact this is hidden as skillfully as it is makes me concerned that none of my answers will come without serious sleuthing.

Sighing, I use the tape to secure the scrap to the puzzle box, and file that under something to ponder later. I go back to sorting the jewelry into separate bins—one for items I'll keep in some sort of armoire furniture thing once I buy it—and one that I'd feel better about storing in a safe. Once that's done, I work my way through the bric-à-brac, carefully weighing each thing based on whether I want to keep it, sell it, or trash it.

Time flies as I methodically whittle my mother's belongings down to a manageable selection, and I stand up to stretch when I hear the truck in the driveway again. That's Gene and the boys, and they'll be taking up space as they carry out the last of the furniture in here and most of the stuff in the two other bedrooms. Grabbing a handful of the correspondence, I ponder for a moment. I don't have to supervise removal since I used colored post-it's marking storage items this morning, so I head downstairs to check on Jekyll and Hyde. It's time for lunch, anyway, and I'm surprised they stayed away for as long as they have.

Their ears perk up as I come into view, and the twin cats leap towards me, flanking both sides immediately. "Hey, guys. You ready for lunch?"

"*Mow!*" Jekyll answers as he trots along with me.

"Yeah, I figured as much."

As has become their routine, they jump onto the counter and sit, waiting for me to toss the various ingredients into the separate mixing bowls I'm using for their food. Humming under my breath as I get them taken care, I move to the fridge again to decide what I'll have. After several minutes of poking, I decide on a sub sandwich and some fruit. I can use some of the fruit for a milkshake, and that would hit the spot after sitting on the floor like a cramped goblin all morning.

I plop down on a stool, munching quietly while the boys chow down. The first bundle of letters I brought seems to be college sweetheart letters between my folks. They're oddly more emotive than I remember my parents being with one another, but everyone's a budding poet in college, I suppose. The next stack relates to estate stuff that may or may not have been taken care of when they passed. I assume it was since my stateside attorney was very thorough, but who knows if there are things he wouldn't have known to look for? I'll have to give that a thorough once over with Jackson once I get settled here. I'm sure he'd drive down from the city to look over anything I find in the next week that concerns me.

Then I hit the motherlode. I almost choke on the bite of sandwich, staring at the bundle I untied in disbelief. It's thick and the papers that comprise the stack are of varying ages—some yellowed with age, some newer looking, and some written on paper so delicate that I'm worried about handling it. Scooting my food and drink aside, I spread the sheets out, sorting them by matching age of the paper. The oldest set appears to be in handwriting I don't recognize, the middle set looks like it might be my dad's, and the newest set is my mother's.

I feel like I keep asking 'what the fuck' but every time I turn around, something weird happens. It's like this town is a nesting doll full of secrets and riddles, and I keep pulling another doll off to reveal a smaller one, except this is never-ending.

Scanning the most recent stack, I frown. They appear to be written in code, though it doesn't look like it's all in the same code. Some sheets use symbols and pictures, some use a mix of words and numbers, and some are a potpourri of all three. Nothing looks even remotely familiar, and I'm fairly decent at cryptography. The first tech company I consulted for when I moved to Europe had me working for the head of their corporate espionage department to ferret out moles, and I had to spend six weeks in a training their new employees took to prepare for it. I won't claim to be a code breaker, but my skills aren't nil.

A quick glance through the other two stacks yields the same results, and I huff in irritation. This is fucking great. Apparently, my parents read too much Tom Clancy or some shit, and now I have to figure out what in the goddamned hell they were doing with old school encrypted documents hidden in their bedroom. Add that to the coded message and the puzzle box and I'm wondering if someone has teleported me into the *Da Vinci Code*.

"Miss Jolene?"

The sound startles me, and I look over at the doorway where one of Niecy's grandsons is standing. "Oh, Ellison. I'm sorry! I got absorbed in some of the stuff I found in my parents' room. What can I do for you? Do you need help?"

He shakes his head, giving me a shy smile. "No, ma'am. Pop-pop wanted me to tell you we have the second load ready to go. We're going to stop near the unit for lunch and then unload. He thinks we'll be able to squeeze one more load in after that before Mimsy wants us home for dinner, but that should finish out the upstairs and the leftovers from the first floor."

Smiling broadly, I walk over to him. "That's fantastic. I'm so grateful to you boys for helping. I tried to hire someone, but Niecy insisted."

"Oh, no, Ma'am. Mimsy would skin us alive if we didn't help you out. She tells everyone that you were her practice grandchild."

Chuckling, I nod. "That she does. Well, let me know if you need anything else. I have two more rooms to sort up there before the end of the day. Gene said you'd come back tomorrow while I'm out to get the trash box stacks."

Ellison nods again and waves, taking off to help his brothers finish loading the truck.

Shit. I should have fed them, right? My mother is probably rolling in her urn right now. I've been pretty good at remembering all the things she taught me since I returned, and I got so wrapped up in this damned mystery that I left my free labor to forage for food. I'll have to call Niecy and apologize for my oversight.

○

Once I clean up the kitchen, I stow the weird documents in my trusty bag and leave it in the care of my fierce new roommates. If I can finish the closet on the master quickly, I can bust through the guest room and the office before Gene's crew returns. I want to be alone when I hit the office because I'm certain it will have more clues hiding amongst my parents' jumbled personal finances, lesson plans, and assorted bullshit that accumulated over two decades of living in this house. Grabbing a rocks glass, I pour a hefty scotch, and head up the stairs.

When I enter the bedroom, I sit my drink down and grab a garbage bag. Most of the clothes will be outdated, but these bags can go to the thrift store outside of town and possibly help someone in need.

I start with my father's clothes, folding and bagging suits, ties, and dress shirts first. There's a small insignia on the French cuffs of the dress shirts he preferred, and I study it for a moment. I've never seen it before, but every single one has it embroidered behind the cufflink holes. Odd. I throw most of the winter clothes in as well, leaving a few oversized jackets and sweaters that I might use for extra warmth when the frost inevitably comes. Pants go next, and again, I keep a few pieces that feel like they might be useful.

If you asked me what for, I couldn't tell you, but my instincts rarely fail me, so I follow them.

Once his side is almost cleaned out, I find another small puzzle box like my mother's sitting beside an onyx box. Grumbling under my breath about my timeline, I ignore the mystery and open the simple box. It contains my dad's pocket watch, several pairs of expensive cufflinks, and a money clip.

Every single one of them have the mysterious logo.

I rub my hand over my face in frustration, knowing the symbol means something, and these are all important items that I need to keep. I close the box, pick its companion up, and take them into the bathroom. Moving the linens aside, I hide the boxes behind them until I can figure where I'm going to store all this valuable mystery shit. It can't be somewhere without safety measures, but it also can't be as far away as the deposit box at the bank I'm going to place my mother's expensive jewels in.

Crime is non existent in the Hollow—save juvenile pranks—but I've seen far too many clients get complacent in the past to let that keep me from making solid choices about security.

Padding back to the closet, I compact the male clothes to the front left area and move over to the side belonging to my mother. Her taste and mine have *never* meshed, so I doubt that I'll be saving much from her wardrobe. Tossing floral atrocities in the bag, I mutter to myself about how I could *possibly* have come out of this woman. One shirt looks like they cut it from a Florida woman muumuu, and I cringe as I fold it. She always looked impeccable and stylish—the latest fashions right off the designer racks—but I was right about much of it being dated, and even more so about it not being my style.

Finally, I hit the last section—zippered garment bags. I'm a little terrified of what Southern lady looking lace monstrosities are stored in these because I may have to sell them if they're vintage and expensive. I'm not in the mood to deal with E-bay, but I can't send clothing valued in the realm of small vehicles to thrift stores. It's not budget savvy.

I pocketed the money in the money clip; you know. Waste not, want not.

When I unzip the first bag, I almost have a fucking aneurism on the spot. The smell of leather assaults my senses and I take a deep whiff, pleasure sparkling through my limbs. Running my fingers over the calfskin, zippers, and studs that adorn it, I look for the tag that will identify who crafted the jacket, pants, and vest in this bag.

Mary Magdalene, mother of whores. It's a motherfucking Saint Laurent—no, not *just* a Saint Laurent. This is hand tailored, Saint Laurent leather motorcycle *set*.

I might have an orgasm from looking at the outfit in this goddamned bag.

Blinking my complete shock out of my eyes, I rush to open the other bags, gasping as couture gowns, skirts, dresses, pants, and shirts of baddest assed variety I've *ever* seen get revealed. What in the absolute *shit* is my mother—patron saint of the Sunday Chanel—doing with this? It's been worn, but well taken care of. Tags hang from the items with locations and dates that I don't recognize, and a band of color that must mean something I don't get yet. There must be over a hundred grand in clothes here—

minimum—and I haven't even figured out where she kept her shoes. I'm drooling just *thinking* about it.

Wait. If my mom had a secret stash of fly clothes, why didn't my dad have something similar?

My eyes close and I try to imagine the past, pushing past the haze in my mind. Work trips. My mother went on work trips for the college to recruit students and staff—several times a year. Dad always stayed with me, joking that he wasn't cut out for the whole 'social networking' aspect of his career.

Could those dates line up with ones my mom went on college recruiting jaunts? I can't remember, and that makes me scream in irritation. My brain has the capacity for infinite amounts of bull crap, but *not* memories of my childhood. It's absolutely baffling.

I finally give in and leave the bags of astounding garments for further perusal later. I won't remember anything right now, and I'm wasting daylight while I stand here and struggle. With the clothes finished, I head for the spare bedroom to work off my frustration on whatever is lying in wait in that mess. I don't think it will hold many secrets, but the office will be last and that I'm banking on holding the keys to the kingdom.

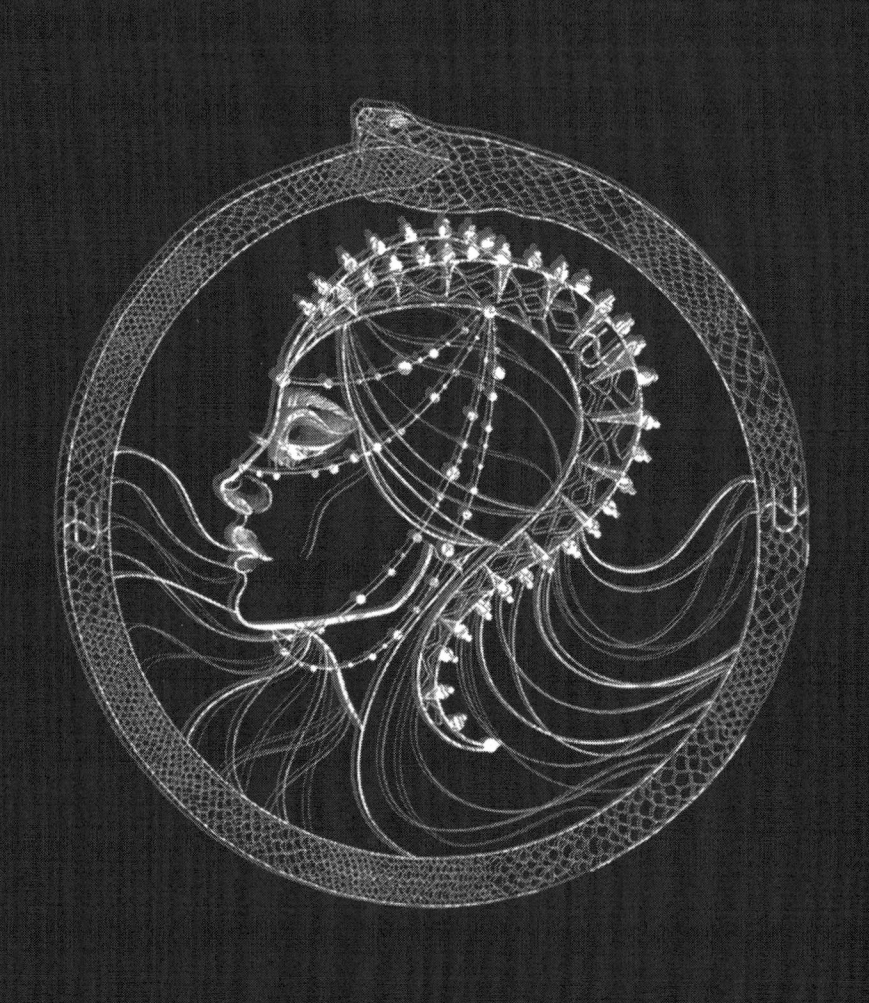

Making Bad Decisions

Jolene

I take back what I said yesterday.

The spare bedroom led to finding what I can only describe as a drool-worthy collection of shoes and a bunch of junk that ended up in the trash stacks. The office was a total bust, and I couldn't be more disappointed by the lack of... anything... that seemed important or mysterious. My only saving grace was that I stored all the documents for later and created a stack of questions for when I have Jackson come down and catch me up on the all the estate shit.

Looking at the computer screen, I sigh. I've been putting off heading towards the farm by spending the last couple of hours ordering furniture, bedding, and all the house shit I'm going to need to make this place mine. Jekyll and Hyde went out in the back for a bit while I did so, hopefully getting out the abundance of energy they woke up with.

According to the internet, it's not uncommon for cats to be lazy as hell and then full of energy, especially a designer breed like those two.

Cleaning up the breakfast mess I'd left, I poke my head out the back door to see them bounding around. I ordered the glasses and about a hundred other idiotic pet owner things for them, but I need to order collars and sensors for a cat door. I'm sure that I can get Gene to install it if I get whatever new-fangled what-sit I find on the 'Zon. I'd like them to have independence. They look at me as if I've called their names before they go back to terrorizing the birds in the landscaping.

I guess it's okay to leave them to their frolicking while I go get ready for this… date.

Jesus. I don't remember the last time I had anything besides an escort to an event or a one-night stand. It's not like I usually have men in my home—My cheeks burn bright red as I remember the other night, and I shake my head to clear it. Edgar was a mistake with a capital 'M' and I'm not going to let that ever happen again. Aggravated and embarrassed, I stride upstairs to throw on clothes suitable for riding horses, vowing to ignore the hot young vet while I get the lay of the land at the Cantwell's farm.

I dig through the boxes stacked in the master, finding the one marked equestrian and pull out what I need. After I lay out my clothes and boots, I head into the bathroom. I refuse to get too dolled up because I'm only going to see the animals. A few swipes with mascara and shadow and a high ponytail later, I feel like I've done enough to appear acceptable if any of the Cantwells are lurking about.

Tugging on a totally unsexy pair of undies that won't chafe, I grin a little. At least I won't get tempted by undergarments while I'm trying not to stare at the smoking hot genius. Boot socks come next, then breeches, dress boots, and finally a tight short-sleeved shirt. I grab my favorite pair of gloves, looking around to make certain I didn't forget anything. Once satisfied, I head downstairs, whistling to call the boys in.

Jekyll and Hyde zoom inside, looking happy and ready to rock. I stuff my gloves into my messenger bag and frown as I put on my sunglasses. Everywhere in town has been accommodating about my shadows coming with me, so I'm going to assume that the Cantwells ranch will be the same. If nothing else, they can run in one field as long as they stay out of hoof range.

"Okay, boys. We're going for a ride. Promise to behave and for the love of everything that's holy, *don't* let me do anything *stupid* this time."

They look at one another, then at me, and if cats could shrug, I'm fairly sure that's what they'd be doing.

Great. Some protectors they are.

○

I pull up to the sprawling horse farm with music streaming from my open windows. My companions are pulling their hyena trick again, and the workers we pass point at them as I slide into a spot in the employee lot. I'm not an employee, obviously, but I plan on helping to exercise the horses, so you could call me a future employee.

That's close enough, right?

Looking at the servals, I put on a stern expression. "So, for real, my dudes. You can get out and roam. People might even feed you—that's all good. All I need you to promise is that you won't kill any of their animals or plants and you won't scare anyone unless they're threatening me. And this gorgeous young vet guy is gonna want to look at you for a few, so let him do it."

They look at me with wide eyes before dipping their heads and letting out a resounding, "*Mow!*"

"Cool. Just be cool and I'll get you nice, thick steaks tonight instead of meatballs. Also... *don't* let me do anything stupid? Please?"

I can't believe I'm asking my erstwhile, uninvited pets to babysit me, but this week has taught me I'm feral and I *do* need watching until I re-integrate into society.

"Mrrrp?" Hyde asks, tilting his head as if that's a silly request.

He's right.

"Yeah, barge in and be cute or something if I'm fucking up. I don't care. Just stop me." Heads bob again, and I sigh, slinging my bag over my shoulder. "Let's rock." Rolling out of the Impala, I adjust my shades and look around.

They filled the entrance to the farm with all the Southern finery of a big house, apple trees, and landscaping—a tour set up, I'd guess. Horse racing is big business in this state, and people come from far and wide near Derby and Keeneland season. They love to tour the Bourbon Trail and the horse farms to get the 'flavor' of the area. I saw the visitor trails, picture perfect fountains and statuary, and the steeples from the road.

However, the employee side of the farm is buzzing with activity. Grooms walking foals, mares, and studs along paths slowly have their heads down as they watch to make sure the expensive horses don't catch their hooves. Stables the size of small houses where they house their prize-winning thoroughbreds and brood stock. On-site housing for trainers, jockeys, grooms, and other staff litters the horizon in the east. Training circles and huge, open fields sprawl for miles to the west. I see a building that looks like it contains the business office and decide it's probably where I should check in. I could go to the stable and ask for directions because I speak a smattering of languages, but that might get me in trouble with the security that is invisible but certainly there.

I whistle at the boys and start towards that building, nodding at the employees I pass. When I open the door, an alarm beeps, causing the svelte woman at the desk to peer over her glasses at me. Squinting, I frown as I work to place her. She's young—about the doc's age—and dressed in what must be a tailor-made uniform of chic designer jeans, a sharp blouse with the farm's name embroidered on it and perfect hair and makeup. She looks vaguely familiar, but given her age, I know I didn't go to school with her.

"Welcome to Cantwell Farms. I'm Agatha Harper Claiborne. May I have your name so I can coordinate with our interview schedule?"

Her tone is polite, but the sweep of her glittering black eyes and sneer on her wine-colored lips says otherwise. Long coffin tipped nails tap on the desk as she waits for my response, and I see right through her façade. I don't know what Agatha wants from life with a glance, but I can guess, and I'm not going to get her closer to a rich, founding family husband, so I must be 'staff'. I've had a rough week, and I decide that fucking with her is good amusement while I wait for my 'date'.

"I don't have an appointment," I say, smiling in the true saccharine way they teach in cotillion classes. Despite Edgar and his cronies ruining the event, I took every class required and strived for excellence to make my mother happy. I can lay it on as well as any bitch in this town, and offering her as little information as possible will set off the 'rude' alarm.

"Tsk," she murmurs, her eyes narrowing with delight. "We don't take walk-ins at Cantwell Farms, *ma'am*."

The stress on the word ma'am tells me she's emphasizing our age difference in the nastiest way she can without being straight up impolite. Too bad for her—I passionately believe that age is a human construct, and I couldn't care less if she's younger than me. "I'm not a walk-in, but thank you for your *kindness*."

Agatha's eyes widen with the return volley, sensing that she won't get rid of me easily, nor will she be able to intimidate me with her typical mean girl act. "*Ma'am*, Cantwell Farms has a security checkpoint at the gate. Did you check-in and state your business when you entered? I will need that information to process your visitor's badge if you're here for a tour."

There's that word again. She's fishing for who let me in without her permission, and I'll be damned if I get a gate guard in trouble. Word of my arrival has spread around town, and I assume cute vet told them to expect me. I gave my name, and the attendant waved me to the employee entrance without a pause. This bitch will get him fired for subverting what must be the only authority she has in life at this desk. So I smile again, walking over to a set of overstuffed chairs across from her dominion. "That's no trouble. I'll wait here until my appointment is available. I'm sure they'll come looking for me soon enough."

A surge of energy crackles through the air as she stands, putting her hand on a cocked, shapely hip. Her lips curve and she bats her lashes slowly, watching me with an intensity that's borderline creepy. "You'll tell me who you're meeting, and I'll give you your badge."

The door alarms buzzes, interrupting our standoff, and I see Hottie McBabyVet coming bustling through with a picnic basket, a blanket, and a bright grin. His eyes light on me and he makes a beeline for where I'm seated.

"Jolene!" He chuckles as he approaches, shaking his head. "It must have been a trial growing up with that name, huh? Every single time I hear it, I want to sing a little ditty from the Tennessee Titan herself."

Laughing, I shrug. "No harder than Wolfgang, I'd imagine."

An annoyed harrumph comes from the desk, and I notice the Vamp Tramp—I mean, Agatha—is coming around the desk towards Wolfie. She looks hungry as a crocodile, and I've been near one or two in Egypt. Every single ounce of her being is oozing sexuality as she approaches him, batting his shoulder with a limp hand. Her glare turns to a pout, and her lashes start up again.

"Oh, Wolfie, darling! You know you're supposed to let me know if you do interviews for the clinic cleaning crew. I must know about all visitors on the property for Mr. Cantwell's records. You don't want to get me in trouble, do you?"

Wincing, the adorable genius backs up from the Vamp Tramp with a gentle smile. "Now, Agatha. I registered her with security and the gate guards myself. She's not on your schedule for staffing because she's both my personal guest and Eliot's. The Cantwell's don't register their *personal* guests with you, do they?"

Her eyes widen and her head whips around to give me a look that would have killed lesser women. Fortunately for me, I've gotten it from mistresses of princes, CEOs, fashion moguls, and various entertainment figures—this small-town tyrant doesn't scare me a whit. Once she sees the satisfaction in my expression as I stare back at her, she turns back to her target with another pout. "I thought *we* would have lunch together again today."

"Sorry, Aggie. Dr. Wolfie and I made this date earlier in the week. I got all gussied up for him and everything, so we'll be on our way. Catch ya on the flip side!"

My 'date' muffles a chuckle with his hand, nodding at the gaping woman in front of him. When he has it under wraps, he gives her a shrug. "She's right. I'm told she has some companions I need to look at, we have to eat, and then we're touring the stables for her commitment to Eliot. We really must get going. Have a lovely day, Agatha!" Grabbing my hand, he gives me a look that says, 'don't you dare pull away' and leads me to the door.

We walk outside and Jekyll and Hyde bound up to us with huge cat grins. I take my hand back, wiping the sudden dampness on my palms on my breeches and clear my throat. "Uh, yeah, sorry about that. No, wait." I frown. "I'm not sorry about her attitude.

Why didn't you warn me there was a viper in the waiting room? This is *your* fault, buster."

Rubbing the back of his head, he blushes—I shit you not—and shrugs. "I try to interact with Agatha as little as possible. She's had this… thing… for me since high school, and it makes everything awkward. Sometimes, I have to be pretty sneaky to get past without getting cornered."

Something in my stomach clenches, and my eyes darken. "That's sexual harassment, and you need to tell HR. Or, since you're close enough to Eliot to call him that, talk to him."

A dour look comes over his face. "He knows. He can't do anything about it because of her family's legacy. They're new for the Hollow in terms of founding families, but their wealth and influence in the racing industry is unparalleled. His parents guaranteed their children job exchanges here to learn the business."

That spot inside clenches again, and I feel rage sparkle through my veins. My work in Europe caused me to be privy to this kind of bullshit in all areas of the ivory tower society, and it made me as angry there as it does here. Business, politics, and even the arts are interwoven with the 'people as commodities' ideology so tightly that anyone who lives that life growing up tends to simply accept it as a fact of their existence. I've gotten myself—and Saoirse—in trouble because of it many times.

That's how Thailand started, in fact.

"That sucks giant goat balls, and I'm sorry you have to deal with her. She didn't bother me because I've dealt with bitchy women WAY above her pay grade for years. She'd have to add quite a few zeroes to her net worth to compete."

His blue eyes sparkle with mirth, and he practically beams at me. "You know, darlin', I think we're gonna get along just fine."

"*Mow!*"

The indignant sound breaks us out of the heated gaze we're

locked in, and I look down at Jekyll. The serval gives me a hopeful look, clearly believing he's done his duty in saving me from doing something stupid. Which I might have if he hadn't spoken up, to be honest. This sexy ass vet might be younger than anyone I've taken for a spin in the past, but his appeal is undeniable. I can feel the attraction in my bones, and I can *not* repeat the mistakes of earlier in the week.

"Are you the scamps that chose our sugarplum? Let me see you, gentleman. Stand and be counted."

As if by magick, the nickname makes me blush and sets me off at the same time. The cats ignore my flustered state as they rise on their hind legs to greet him. Both Jekyll and Hyde offer opposing paws to him, and my jaw drops. Jekyll lets out one of his trademark yowls, and Hyde makes a low 'Mrrrrp' as Wolfie walks around them, inspecting their forms like an art connoisseur.

"I... they don't normally..."

Looking up from where he's checking parts of them I've been studiously avoiding, he winks at me. "I'm a vet, sugarplum. Animals love me." When he stands again, he picks up the basket and blanket he'd been holding inside. "The good news is that they seem healthy, though I'd like to do a full exam later in the month once you're fully settled. The bad news is that Hyde is a girl, and they aren't fixed."

I blink for a moment, feeling the blush on my cheeks get even redder. How could I fuck up something as simple as gendering my fucking pets? Goddess, I must look like an absolute fool. Why didn't those idiots tell me?

Holy hell, this town is making me lose my marbles. I seriously just asked myself why my cats didn't tell me their gender.

"Um... well, I'm not going to do that to them. They're a bonded pair, it seems, and I don't feel like I should make that decision for them. It feels like I'd be intruding on their privacy."

His grin spreads further, and he nods, which I don't expect. "I agree! So many people want to prevent their companions from living normal lives to make it easier for them. I applaud your willingness to allow them autonomy, sugarplum. I'll help you get what supplies you may need when I do their visit."

Breathing a sigh of relief that I seem to have passed that unintentional test, I nod. "That sounds good. Should we have lunch? I don't want to keep you all day."

"Oh! Yeah, we should. I have a slow day today, but I bet you're itchin' to get to your studio and work a little. Word at the diner is that you've stripped the house pretty bare."

My nose wrinkles and I sigh. Bloody country gossips—as much as I love Niecy and Gene, they've been keeping everyone informed about everything I've been doing. It's a good thing that I didn't ask about any of the sketchy stuff I've found in the house. I have no idea who or what could be involved in this mystery of mine. I can't play my hand before I see the table and count the cards.

"I am. I want to make sure the equipment is installed properly so once I get my feet under me at school, I can start lessons and showings there."

Wolfie grabs my hand again, leading me to a golf cart nearby. "I'm going to take us out to a spot the tourists don't get to see, if you don't mind. We'll eat there, and if it's late when we finish, we can do the stables tour later. Eliot instructed Fidelia to make you a badge, a parking decal, and shirts and have 'em delivered to your house so next time you can just text me and head on over."

As I plop down in the cart with my bag, I wave at Jekyll and Hyde. They're clearly electing to slink around here, and I can't say that's a bad idea. If Eliot really put me on the payroll officially, people will need to get used to them being around while I'm here. Plus, who knows what secrets they can ferret out and lead me to later? I'll bet those two are better sleuths than they let on.

"So, Eliot's folks still hold the reins—literally. He's the go-between for the staff and the family, but he can't pry the title out of his daddy for anything. It makes him crazy because he has tons of innovative ideas for modernization that would not have included back handed deals like the one with Agatha's family. He's got contacts in the Middle East, which I'm sure you know is a hotbed for sheikhs with money to burn on luxury items like racehorses."

I snort. I *definitely* know that. "Yep. I've been around that scene enough to know how shark infested those waters are, though. There's a lot of protocol involved, and he'll need a cultural liaison to help the deals go smoothly and not get outwitted by their London barristers."

He navigates the cart over bumps and hills before he turns and gives me that sexy megawatt smirk. "Word on the farm is that he heard a certain sugarplum might help with that. I think that's why he was eager enough to get you squared away on his payroll—even starting out as a horse helper—before some other founding family approached you for their own business dealings."

Motherfucker. Talk about sharks in the goddamned water. Wolfie is telling me that every family in the Hollow will try to lure me out of art and teaching for globe trotting consulting. That's not my plan and I'd better make that clear now.

"Well, I came here to settle down for a while, Wolfie. I've lived the life of the glamorous fixer for years, and when I moved back to the States, I set that aside for other dreams. That eventually led me back home to the Hollow. They'll be disappointed if they think money will get me to hop on their jets to negotiate their troubles."

"I told Aldous that yesterday, but he was quite smug in his assertion that he and the mayor are very persuasive. Though, he had Poe and Parker with him and when he schemes with those sphinxes in his arms, my brain goes straight to a Southern Dr. Evil, and I almost laugh in his face."

The image that flits through my head is hysterical and I giggle, doubling over as he finally pulls the cart to a stop beneath a tree with an old rope swing under it. The meadow is lovely and far enough out from the commotion of the main area of the farm that I doubt anyone would even know we're here. I wipe my eyes as I take in the bucolic scenery that horse country offers with a sigh. I didn't know how much I missed this amount of green until just now.

Wolfie climbs out, spreading the blanket in a spot under the tree that looks made for it, and sits down the basket. I watch him fiddle with the food and drinks with a smile, his touch of compulsiveness for neat presentation very fitting for the town he lives in. He stands, raising one arm as he scratches his stomach, and the butterflies start in mine as I watch.

Good goddamn, he's hot.

Holding his hand out, he helps me out of the cart, and I flush again. His lips brush my knuckles so quickly I think I imagine it, but the wink he gives me after confirms his flirting. I suck in a breath, completely caught off guard when a quick bang for posterity isn't the goal, but I follow him to the vast blanket. Lowering myself to the ground, I settle, and my eyes flit around nervously.

I didn't mention that I'm a picky eater and this might have been a terrible plan.

○

"So, the whole thing ended up being a *complete disaster* and my mother was furious with me as if I'd arranged the popular kids pulling one of the meanest pranks in the history of the Hollow," I finish sheepishly, sipping a glass of the champagne he was kind enough to bring.

Wolfie grins, shaking his head and his sun kissed skater cut falls in his eyes. "I had *no idea* you were part of the 'Cotillion Catastrophe'. People talk about it at the start of every season, but they only whisper. They never mention names before some old biddy shushes them as if speaking it aloud could will it into existence again."

My face turns bright red. "Well, I'm sure they're terrified that some dumbass kids will try to re-create it. Edgar, Ophelia, Benjy, Reese, Jillian, Amy, Blake, Dylan, and their cronies on the football and cheer squads made sure that it was legendary. I know I'll never forget it."

His amusement flits away like a leaf on the breeze, and the hottest young vet I've ever seen scoots closer to me. A hand comes up to cup my jaw and he murmurs, "Sugarplum, I can promise you I'd kick Edgar square in the nuts if it'd make you smile after that story."

Ducking my head in embarrassment, I try to get myself under control. Something about Wolfie makes me both shy and ready to devour him at the same time and I haven't the foggiest how to respond. The conversation until now was easy and light, paired with food that I loved, and good bubbly. I'm not sure what to do now that it's taken a turn towards the intimate.

Don't shite where ye lie, Saoirse would say.

However, if she could SEE the sculpted underwear model in front of me, she'd change that tune right quick. I know my bestie, and good sense has never impeded a fun time when she's around. Hence ending up in the middle of a Southeast Asian scandal and a smuggled exit from a country I'd love to visit again someday.

"It's okay. I mean, I won't forget, but it doesn't actively hurt me anymore. You know how the politics in this town go—I don't think it was about me. I got in the way, and I was collateral damage. I've stood in front of the firing squad to protect people who can't protect themselves and that was one of those times."

He scoots closer, his face inches from mine as he tips my chin back up to look into those baby blues. "I like that about you, sugarplum. In fact, I like a lot of things about you."

I respond, but his lips meet mine before I can. A surge of intense need fills me, and I push forward, crawling over his form like I've done it million times. His chest rumbles with a growling sound, and I pull back slightly, grinning against his mouth. The air feels charged with energy like it did with Edgar, and I nip his lower lip, tugging on it with my teeth. Our bodies shift, landing in perfect harmony, and groans echo through the silence of the field.

"You're offering yourself to me, little Wolfie?"

His hands slide over my ass, squeezing playfully as he smirks back at me. "Are you accepting, Jolene Athena Whitley?"

Using my full name strikes me as important, but I nod. "I am, Wolfgang Lucien Fletcher."

"We've been drinking," he murmurs, his eyes meeting mine as if to check my level of intoxication. His expression is serious, but he's so goddamned cute that I feel like I could gobble him up on the spot.

One of my shoulders lifts and falls as I bob my brows. "Not enough to make a difference in my thought process. Or are you all bark and no bite?"

His eyes widen for a second as he looks at me, and I wonder what he's seeing. I know that I'm not a bloody fashion hound like the women here, and I'm thinner than I was in high school, but still on the curvy side. Is he regretting his flirting already?

"Look, if you don't want—"

My self-conscious babble is cut off by hands whipping the

tight riding shirt over my head and flinging it aside. I push up on my hands, wiggling until I can help him push the knee-high boots off as well. His boots are next, and I giggle when he gets his scrub shirt off with some serious maneuvering. I find out that scrub pants are my new favorite pants when they come untied and slide right off, leaving him looking like the fucking Calvin Klein model I thought he was in his boxer briefs.

"You're going to have to get those damned breeches loose, sugarplum. I'm aware of how tightly they cling to legs like yours." His eyes dance as he leans up to kiss me briefly, giving me room to figure out my riding pants.

"Son of a bitch," I mutter, wishing for the millionth time that I had magick powers to help me with shit like this. My hips bump and wriggle against his, eliciting groans of approval as I get the tight pants over my badonkadonk and down my legs far enough for us both to fight them down my legs. When they're finally kicked aside, I pump my fist in victory and he laughs along with me.

His eyes travel down my body and mortification thrums in my veins when I remember I wore *functional* undergarments for riding today, *not* sexy ones, and now he knows. My head falls, the ponytail full of my thick hair hiding my bright red face.

Oh, sweet lord Hades, claim me now. I'm ready to exit this planet because this super fucking sexy, smart guy has seen my lady boxers and body wrapped sports bra.

"Jolene? Sugarplum? What's wrong?"

I lift my head, blowing strands of hair out of my face. "So. Embarrassing."

He frowns, his hands sliding up my back to my shoulder blades as he looks at me. "What's embarrassing?"

"I'm dressed like a confused granny mummy!"

Wolfie chuckles, then bursts out laughing as he looks up at me.

"You're dressed like a woman who knows how to ride like a pro. If I'd found a thong and a lacy wisp under here, I never could have taken you seriously with my horses again."

Blinking, I tilt my head. "Really? This isn't like… a major turn off? My boobs are bound, and I have on lady boxers."

"Women who dress for function and form are sexy as fuck, sugarplum. I'm a vet—I can't deal with a lady who'd get grossed out if I came home covered in unmentionable gunk."

An actual shit-eating grin blossoms on my face, and I reach down to tug on the clip of my binding. Wolfie unfurls the wrap the rest of the way, unzips the sports bra and tosses it, his hips bumping into mine enticingly as he does so. Once I'm bare, his eyes roam over the tattoo wrapping around my ribs, the belly ring, and of course, the jeweled silver and emerald shields I sport on my nipples. Saoirse is to thank for most of it, as she can talk me into anything when we're drunk. But Edgar liked it, and it looks like my darling vet does as well.

I might send her a candy basket.

"Sugarplum, I don't think the first time is gonna last awfully long. You're dolled up like a pin-up girl in a tattoo mag under here. It's making my dick do backflips."

"What, country girls around here don't have body piercings and tats?" I tease. I slide my pussy over the material of his boxers, my eyes rolling back into my head at the friction. He's right, of course. The ordeal with our clothes should have dumped ice water on our heads, but his acceptance of me only fanned my flames hotter.

His fingers pinch my ass in reprimand, and I scoot down his thighs, nipping at his delicious abs as I go. He tries to wriggle away, but now I've decided that I'm on a mission. If the first time will be quick, I'm going to show him how fast I can make it.

Biting down on the waistband of his boxers, I tug the material down with my teeth until his cock springs free.

Well, butter my biscuits and call me *Betty Crocker*—I hit the jackpot.

He's got a sexy ass ladder on that thick shaft of his, and his pelvis is covered in intricate tats of his own. They look vaguely Gaelic, but I'm too excited about my dicks-covery to scrutinize them. Leaning in, I inhale his scent, pleased to find that he smells like body wash and outdoorsy man, not sweaty horse guy. That alone deserves a treat. So I lick the tip lightly and he shudders from head to toe.

Oh, this will be fun. I think Wolfie likes me in charge.

Swallowing him in one deep motion, I run my tongue over the bars, flicking them in a way I know will feel good. It's not my first rodeo with a pierced dude, but they always have different versions of how they want you to play with their steel. I bob up and down slowly, humming a bit as I learn what spots make him gasp and squirm. If you're wondering, I've had lessons, and I'm a fair bloody hand at this, but I don't do it for everyone.

However, Hottie McBabyVet can ask nicely annnnytime.

I suppress a giggle when I feel his hips jump and I go back to work, licking, sucking, and teasing until I can feel his frame tense. He mutters something about moving, but I bat his hands away, giving him one more nip at the tip as it passes through my lips. The orgasm must hit him like a brick to the face because he shouts so loud that I worry someone's going to hear, and salty fluid fills my mouth. When I can feel his breathing even out, I give him one last kiss, sliding up his body like the cat that blew the canary.

Which I did, thank you very much, and he should praise me for it.

"Holy Horned God, Jolene. Where in the hell did you—never

mind, I don't wanna know. Just... give me a few and we're back, sugarplum."

I arch a brow at him. "A few?"

His grin spreads wider. "Darlin', I'm only twenty-two. I definitely meant a few."

This time my eyes fly wide, and I squeal as he flips me onto my back.

What have I gotten myself into?

○

"Hello, there, guys," I say, looking at Jekyll and Hyde with a disapproving look.

They lift their heads from the bowls of lunchmeat they're munching with guilty expressions. Several of the hands' kids, and a bunch of tour folk, are watching them in fascination and now I know why they weren't available to save me from myself.

They found people to feed and lavish attention on them.

Some wing... cats... they are.

"Uh, sugarplum?" Wolfie asks, walking up behind me. He picks a piece of grass out of my hair, and I know I turn beet colored as the tourists laugh and whisper.

"Goddamnit," I mutter. "Must I always look like an idiot in public in this town?"

He drops a kiss on my temple and takes the basket out of the cart. "Well, if it's with me, I can't say I'd complain."

"*Wolfgang Lucien Fletcher!*"

The shriek catches us and the crowd off guard, but my faithful companions leap into action. Jekyll and Hyde spring from the bowl of meat towards the blonde woman that is striding over as if she's the Fifth Infantry mounting a surprise attack. Agatha is so intent on screeching at my most recent lover that she doesn't notice them, and they hit her in unison, causing her to totter on her ridiculously high-heeled boots.

"*Ahhhh*! I'm being *attacked* by vicious monsters!"

I roll my eyes at the crowd, hoping to calm them, and follow Wolfie to where my now forgiven wing-cats are pinning the shrieking banshee to the ground with snarls. Taking a chance, I decide on German because I'm hoping to figure out if they've been trained with actual commands. "Jekyll! Hyde! *Mach Schnell!*"

Their heads raise and they bound to my side immediately, still sneering and growling at the prone woman. Agatha doesn't make a move to get up, only continues wailing as if someone has fatally wounded her. Wolfie looks at me and shrugs, and I shrug back. I don't know what the hell she's playing at.

"They've broken my *ankle*! *Help*!"

"Uh, doubtful, you cotton headed ninny. If it's broken, it's those idiotic heels are to blame, not my cats," I call, giving the photo snapping crowd a wink.

A chuckle escapes the band of lookie-loos, and soon the entire group of people roars with laughter. They only part when a large, beefy looking man in a suit comes bounding through like a juggernaut. My lips quirk when I realize who it is, and I continue to watch the hapless bint flail about like a trout out of water.

"What in the sweet baby Jesus is goin' on 'round here?" Agatha stops her caterwauling when the booming voice echoes off the buildings like Moses came down from the Mount. "Who's havin' a hissy fit in the middle of my parking lot?"

I raise my hand and wave, unconcerned about my messy appearance, as Eliot James Cantwell comes striding towards me with a grin. He's dressed in a bespoke summer suit, matching boots, and a straw fedora that makes him look every bit the Southern gentleman that he was raised to be. His parents were friends with mine, and they graciously allowed me to ride their less valuable horses when I was younger. Eliot was always more involved in the farm than Fidelia, and despite being older than me, he's the one who taught me to ride. I wouldn't say we're besties or anything, but he's taken a shine to me since I was a chubby kid in braids.

"Miss Jolene Athena Whitley, I declare you are a *sight* for sore eyes!"

My brow arches when he lays the Southern on thick for the crowd, but I walk over and accept the giant bear hug he offers. It's more friendly than I assumed we were, but this may all be for show. He has guests watching this minor scene, and the Cantwells are all born with an innate sense of public decorum. "Hi, Jamie. It's been a while."

Agatha looks up from the ground, her eyes full of fear, when she hears the nickname for her boss. She must have figured out that I'm not a rando tramp thwarting her day, and now she's regretting her life choices.

Good.

"It sure has, darlin'. Is Wolfgang here showing you a fun time? Getting you loosened up for the task?"

Wolfie chokes, covering his mouth to hide a chortle, and I roll my eyes again. Men, no matter what age, can *not* resist a pussy or dick joke, even in front of their boss. I scratch my chin, pretending to consider, but I eventually smile at Eliot.

"He's done an excellent job at preparing me for regular riding."

The blonde on the ground struggles to her feet, picking hay off of her uniform as she does so. "Mr. Cantwell. I'm sorry to inform you, but those beasts of hers attacked me. I won't feel safe with them or her frequenting these grounds. We'll have to let Mayor Cornelia know so she can decide about their status."

Whipping around to glare at the bitch, I grind out, "Jamie, they only jumped on her because she was screaming and coming towards Wolfie and I threateningly. I called them off, and this entire crowd of tourists has gotten an eyeful of an employee having a complete meltdown in public. I have thirty plus witnesses to her little display." He looks at me for a moment, and then eyes the poor, trapped tour as they nod and murmur agreement. "Also, Agatha, I'd prefer if you didn't discuss someone deciding my companions' *status* as if that doesn't imply that they will be *killed* for accidentally knocking you over in those ridiculous stilts."

A sound of horror erupts from the group. Goddess bless him, I hear a kid ask his mom if the mean lady is going to have the nice kitties murdered. I'd buy that kid a fucking Xbox if I knew who the hell it was.

"Eliot," Wolfie interrupts. "I'm a veterinarian. I wouldn't allow feral animals to roam unattended on this farm. Jekyll and Hyde were wandering the grounds for hours, unattended, and the worst they did was accept a bunch of food and pets. Agatha scared them, and you know how companions get when their person is in danger."

The big man claps his hands and smiles widely. "Well, that's certainly true. Agatha, let's get you to medical while young Wolfie checks Jolene's cubs to make certain they weren't harmed. Carol will take the tour group to the bar for drinks."

"I won't have her and those *beasts* stalking me!"

That was a mistake—a huge one.

"Now, sugar, I don't think you intend to cause a scene on my farm, now do you? Your father would be most displeased if you embarrassed your family in public. I'll take you to medical and tell you what... Jolene and her companions don't have to come by the office ever again. I'll have Fidelia upgrade her pass to permanent salaried, and we'll call that even."

Agatha looks ready to murder me as she takes Eliot's hand, and I let out a breath. I don't know what bargain I just made with the devil to save cats I didn't even HAVE four days ago, but it looks like the crossroads have been crossed.

I can only hope to hell that I don't regret it.

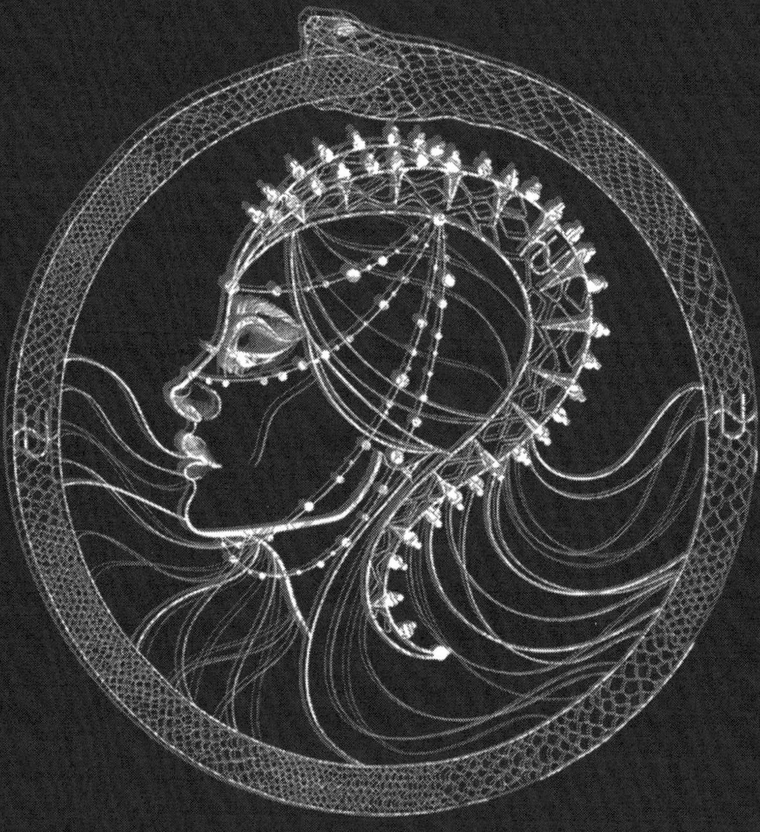

Famous in a Small Town

Jolene

After another grievous error in judgement at the farm, I load up the kitties and head for town. If I'm lucky, I'll make it to the school before the news of the drama makes it to the gossips. I'd prefer not to get the 'looks' that the biddies in the office always seem to give young people enjoying their lives. It's like they're dried up prunes and they think we're inviting Satan himself to host a rave if we get seen without sleeves. My temper can't handle Judgy Judies today—not after the junior version of that trope made a scene that's sure to make the front page of the *Hollar* gossip pages this week.

Pulling into the parking lot of my alma mater is strange this far from matriculation. I feel a sense of belonging, yet a sense of separation that makes me uncomfortable. I don't know if that's because of my tenuous relationship with memories of my past or if it's normal for graduates to experience an uneasiness at returning to the place where the worst years of their life happened.

Don't 'at' me on that—very few people have positive high school experiences. I'm not being a bitter Millennial; high school is four to six years of bullying, trauma, hormones, and an ache for freedom that adults aren't ready to grant. Even the most lenient parents set boundaries that reflect the world as they grew up, not as teens are experiencing it currently. It sets them all up for battles and misery when paired with the Draconian social caste systems that student bodies develop.

Oh, yeah, my degree is definitely in clinical psych, right?

Stepping out of the Impala, I bend to grab my bag and unbuckle my companions. A piercing wolf whistle makes the hairs stand up on the back of my neck, and I bolt upright. Narrowly missing clonking my head, I whip around to shout a scathing response to the misogynistic fuckwit who thought behaving like an old timey cartoon character was cool.

Only I find a group of teenage boys that appear to be about the age of juniors standing with their hands on their jocks and tossing a football back and forth.

You have *got* to be motherfucking kidding me. I could be their 'MTV young' mother, for Aphrodite's sake.

Jekyll and Hyde bound out of the car, clearly sensing my discomfort, and land on either side of me with glares on their whiskered faces. The boys' eyes widen and they guffaw, still eyeing me like a piece of meat. A cougar I am not—despite my tryst with Hottie McBabyVet today—and I roll my eyes, flicking my ponytail over my shoulder to show my dismissal of their moronic behavior.

I'm so focused on pointedly ignoring their catcalls as I walk to the door. It doesn't occur to me that the football team is Edgar's domain and that might mean—

"Well, hello, sugar."

I goddamned swear, the Universe is plotting against me.

Turning on my heel, I face the escape artist himself. I cross my arms over my chest, letting Jekyll and Hyde do their protective snarls without a word of chastisement. He deserves ALL of our wrath for deserting me without so much as a 'Sorry I broke your bed' note. "Hello, Edgar. Are those your little doppelgängers?"

His brow arches and he glances over his shoulder where his JV O-line is still hooting and hollering in my direction. Jerking a thumb at them, he smirks. "Them? Just boys, *drugar*." He lifts his fingers to those lush lips and blows a whistle that makes even MY ears scream before facing the hyena squad. "We. Do. *Not*. Harass. Women. Gentleman! 50 *laps for the entire team. Now*!!"

The boys look like they've seen a ghost, moving like The Flash on his treadmill in the field's direction. I can't hear what they're saying, but I bet they're terrified. Domination Edgar is also Coach Edgar, and those boys have *no* idea what they're dealing with.

"Better?"

I sniff, shrugging. "I suppose." Spinning around again, I march towards the door and give him my back. I refuse to let him know how much seeing him is affecting me, and I don't want to have the discussion we need to have in public. He doesn't comment, but I can feel his eyes on my back as I open the doors and head for the office.

Why can't one damned thing be simple in this blasted town?

○

"Why, Jolene, it's *so* nice to meet you! I've heard such *lovely* things about you!"

I blink at the very blonde, brightly colored, very Southern woman that is Bobbi Jo Ratliff. I'd spoken to her on the phone several times in my various interviews, but nothing could have prepared me for the woman in person. She's like someone took an older Elle Woods, dumped her in Pulitzer instead of Prada, bleached her hair an almost silver platinum, and gave her the personality of Kathy Najimy.

She's also a hugger.

Damn Edgar. That motherfucker should have warned me. I bet he's laughing in his stupid, ass hugging athletic shorts. Yes, yes! I noticed.

"Um, well, it's nice to meet you, too, Principal Ratliff."

Her laugh booms in the wood paneled office, echoing like a funhouse. I don't even want to KNOW what it sounds like in here when she loses her temper. "Oh, Jolene! We don't stand on tradition like my predecessor did. Whistler's Hollow Finishing School is *remarkably different* that when you attended under Principal Masterson."

I'll have to see that to believe it, to be honest. "That sounds good, ma'am—I mean, Bobbi Jo. I didn't have a truly terrible experience here as some alumnae might have, but every institution can benefit from sweeping changes over the years."

Her bright magenta lips break into a wide smile, and she nods. "That's *just* what I told the board when I took over. We no longer require a uniform—that was my first decision, and I stand by it. Those old stuffy shirt academy type clothes only made for teens with little outlet for their emotions and it contributed to poor decorum. We have rules about attire for minors, obviously, but the staff and students dress casually. Only if they violate our simple guidelines, do they lose the privilege and get relegated to business casual."

Hell motherfucking yes. I could kiss this ridiculous woman.

"Does that mean that I can wear clothing that is appropriate for creating art in my classroom? Nothing scandalous, of course, but not 'teacher wear'? And I can encourage my students to bring art-friendly clothes that stay within your code for classes?"

"Of *course*! It would be patently idiotic to have those little darlings ruining Gucci with oil paint, don't you think?"

I roll my eyes. Their name brand extravagance wasn't my

concern, but if Bobbi Jo will let them dress for class, then I don't have to worry about parents throwing hissies about ruined Armani, either. It's a win-win, even if she doesn't get *why* I want students to have the freedom to be messy. "I do, Bobbi Jo. I appreciate your vote of confidence."

"Since you've filled out all your paperwork, would you like a tour of the building? We've made several upgrades, including the art wing."

Art wing? What in the actual fuck?

"I would adore that, Bobbi Jo, but I need to get more chores out of the way before the staff meeting Monday. I've got my house moderately under control, but I need to check in on the studio installations, and I have to get my syllabus together as well."

"*Too cute!*" she yells. "Honey, if you show up with everything done, you'll be the talk of the meetin'. I can only think of one other teacher who will be that prepared."

You can bet your ass it isn't Coach Edgar.

"Well, I like to get off on the right foot, ma'am." I hold my hand out, wincing when she grabs me into another bone crushing bear hug. "I'll email you if I have questions while I'm logging in this weekend."

"You do that, honey!"

Backing away as quickly as I can without looking like I'm running, I find Jekyll and Hyde sitting on the bench outside the office. They give me a quizzical look and I shudder, hoping to convey that they did NOT want to be on the receiving end of the principal's affections.

"Okay, my dudes. Time to check out the installations and do a little unpacking."

Walking around the edge of the room, I envision the walls painted, the floors polished, and the logo emblazoned on the front window. The space is airy, but intimate, and I'll want to add to the tastefully recessed lighting for both form and function. I'm lucky enough to have a storefront that isn't facing the sun, though I'll have the inside glass coated with a UV protectant, regardless. I can't have the light damaging the art while it's being shown.

I pull out my phone, opening my project management app and start making notes about which contractors to call in which order. I'll start with lighting, as wrought iron pieces that look SoHo rustic will stand out in a town like this. After that, I can have the flooring upgraded to a matte black finish and add a coat of paint to the walls in a neutral color. I'll switch out the bulbs to art friendly lighting and have dimmers and event strobes hidden in discreet corners. I'll need supplies for mounting and lighting individual pieces on the walls, and equipment for displaying 3D installations as well. Furniture is on the list as well, since I'll need a small reception podium, seating, and tables for when we host events.

Frowning at the list, I slot in a call to Jackson to sort the estate leftovers out, as I haven't touched my inheritance funds since my parents passed, and I'll need it for seed money. I need him to draw up incorporation papers, handle licensing, and re-jigger all the accounts to keep the I.R.S. from blackballing me as well. He's going to be busy for a couple months; I hope he's ready.

Once I settle the list of supplies for the gallery portion, I walk into the back room. It's much bigger than the front, considering I require art storage space, a working studio, an office, and a lesson space for the students. I was lucky a space as large as this was open on such brief notice, but as I walk through the rooms, I can tell that it's perfect. The installers have painted the walls in a neutral color; the floors are all a dull concrete with drains, and my equipment appears to be in working order. The sinks work, the wheel is functioning, and all my personal tools organized in the exact diagram I provided, including the supply storage areas.

Adding a list of actual materials to order for myself and the studio, I walk into the office. It's bare, but the cool black marble I picked coordinates with the soft purple walls as planned. Saoirse swore I was decorating it like a Vegas bordello, but purple is my favorite color and I like the seductive atmosphere it creates. I make an entry for office furniture on the list and walk out, sighing in relief.

I have no idea if Bobbi Jo will let me use the kiln at the school, but my guess is she won't mind. That lifted a HUGE weight off my shoulder. I wonder what other fancy devices they might have in their new 'art wing'. I'm trained in a lot of mediums, and I love to learn new ones. Having the rich assholes in the Hollow pay for that with their taxes feels quite satisfactory if I say so myself.

"*Mow!*"

The cats come skidding in on the highly polished floor and I laugh. Time to add studio shoes to that idiotic pet owner list. They need to be protected from any dangerous things lurking in a functioning art studio. I'll have to teach them about what they can sniff or lick, too. That's going to be interesting.

"Well, they didn't fuck it up, guys. I'm as shocked as you."

Hyde bobs her head, looking at me with wide eyes before darting her gaze back to the doorway. Jekyll lets out another yowl and I tilt my head. They're trying to tell me something.

"Jolene! I'm so happy I caught you. Did your contractors get everything set up correctly? I must confess that I recommended them to your attorney when he called to complete the lease."

Mayor Cornelia Sykes is standing in the doorway to the studio. I hear a deafening roar come from the front of my building and I freeze, a look of terror on my face. Jekyll and Hyde tense up on either side of me, their bodies preparing for defense as the loud noise gets closer. Finally, the Mayor winks at me, moving to the side of the doorjamb to allow a motherfucking LION to stand beside her.

My jaw drops to the floor, and I do my best Shemp routine as my servals hiss like they're ready to attack the king of the goddamned jungle to protect me. "That's—That's…"

Her rich laugh tumbles from her full lips, and her braids touch the base of her spine as her head tips back. The lion shakes his mane. His eyes narrow on my companions suspiciously, but he doesn't advance. When Nelia finally gathers herself, she wipes her eyes, giving me an amused smile. "Oh, Jolene, I haven't laughed that hard in a long time. You looked like you were going to have a coronary on the spot."

"It's a fucking *lion*!" I manage.

"Yes, yes, he is," she replies, her fingers checking her colorful makeup carefully for streaks, as if she can see her face. She looks down at Jekyll and Hyde with a fond expression. "It's okay, little ones. Zareb will not harm you. He is friendly with all the companions in town, whether furred, feathered, scaled, or otherwise."

I look down at the crew, shrugging. "If Nelia says he won't harm us, we'll have to trust him. The roar was misleading, though."

Cornelia laughs again, shaking her head. "Zareb despises when I leave him in the car. I leave the window open, of course, but he prefers to be near my side. I simply didn't want to frighten you, but he clearly had other plans."

My eyes narrow as I look at the fierce beast, and his head drops as if to acknowledge that he misbehaved. Jesus, the animals in this town are drinking the same magic fucking water as the hot dudes. They act like humans, and I'm not even going to broach why serious predators are allowed to roam freely about the city. "Well, since I've been scared out of my wits and we've calmed our kitties down, how can I help you? I was planning to come to Town Hall next to drop in like you asked."

"I wanted to verify my contractor completed your work satisfactorily, and I brought you the license for your companions. I had Aldous expedite it without you present—in case you got caught up in your unpacking—and though he complained, he finished this morning."

Her lips quirk and I realize the mayor knows her executive assistant is an odious little toad, but she allows it because he's good at his job. Taking the papers she offers while giving Zareb a cautious side-eye, I nod. "Thank you, Nelia. That was on my list for Town Hall and now you've saved me a trip. The work is amazing, to answer your question, and I'd love to have the contact information for a few other workers to help finish this place."

She fishes in the pocket of her wildly colorful pantsuit, handing me her card. "My email is on here, and if you'll let me know what you need, I'll send along information. I appreciate you wanting to use local workers instead of having your attorney send city folk. It helps the economy, and it makes your new business look Hollow-friendly."

I beam. "I've always been a shop local when I can type of gal. Of course, sometimes that's not possible because of availability or the... attitude of certain people... but I promise I will when I can, ma'am."

Tutting at my accidental use of ma'am, Nelia nods as she looks around. "You'll be having lessons for students and showings. Have you considered partnering with Hazel and perhaps Benjy for some of those... drink and draw or paint and eat type events? I think many of the women here would love to have some wine at the bar and paint little keepsakes for their homes."

A snort escapes and I cover my mouth. As if these people who own *actual* Monets and Rembrandts would want to display homemade claptrap in their modern-day mansions. "I... uh, that never..."

Amusement flits over her caramel skin and she shakes a finger at me. "Now, Jolene. Just because people are wealthy doesn't mean they don't enjoy doing 'normal' things on their own occasionally. It's good business sense to cater to their need for being 'one of the little people' and showing off for their other wealthy friends."

I blink. She has me there. To that end, I could do craft classes with Dylan in his bookshop or teach yoga or self-defense classes in the park. The nearest gym is twenty minutes out of town if the traffic is good, and I'd bet most of them simply use Pelotons or something equally expensive in their homes instead of making the trip. All those things will expose me to gossip and chatter without having to interrogate, and no one would be the wiser.

Now I know why Nelia has been mayor since I was in high school—the woman is savvy as hell. She's also possibly drinking from the ruddy Fountain of Youth, but that's a puzzle for another day.

"That gives me great ideas, Nelia. I don't need to charge much —money's not the issue now—but it would help me re-acquaint myself with the town. I appreciate your input," I reply.

"Well, Zareb and I have a few more stops to make before we need to be at Town Hall for meetings. Please contact me for that info, and anything else you need. Have a lovely day, Jolene." The lion turns tail and heads into the front as she winks at my own companions, then exits in a trail of spicy perfume.

Looking down at Jekyll and Hyde, I whisper, "That was weird, right?"

"*Mow!*" they reply in unison.

"Yeah, super fucking weird. She showed up before I could find her, and she's accompanied by a bloody lion. Just when I thought this place couldn't get any stranger..."

After I finished up at the studio, I went to Atwater's and loaded up on groceries. Going into town for meals or DoorDashing stuff is a short-term solution, and now that I'm living in a functional home like a real girl, I gotta start cooking again. I've been far too complacent with my routine since that stupid agent gave me the brush off. I didn't spend my college years studying while on the bike and treadmill to go back to the body I hated as a teen. I'm not 'skinny'; in fact, I'm definitely a mid-sized curvy woman and I've learned to love this shape without developing an eating disorder.

Plus, if I'm going to be banging that hot little vet on the regular, I need to be comfortable in my skin. Wolfie seemed to appreciate my curves, and even that jackwad Edgar didn't act like the teenaged twit he used to be about my nakedness. I'm a straight eight in Europe, but they have different body standards than Americans do. I can't help but get a little nervous when I remember the hurts in my past.

Okay. Enough moping. I'm an adult now, and my high school shit needs to stay in the past where it belongs, even here. Besides, what am I doing acting like I'm going to hop on the Teddy train and take another blind ride? He's on my shit list for the foreseeable future, and people are going to wag their tongues like puppies after word of my romp with the town vet gets around. I can't start building a fucking harem.

Although, there are a few other sexy specimens floating around...

Oh my god, what is *wrong* with me?!!!

Saoirse would cackle her tits off at this line of thought, and she'd be right to do so. I've never successfully dated *one* guy. My pathetic attempt after my weight loss in college ended in betrayal and a pain so deep that I started dating women when I moved to

Paris for my first consulting job. They were hot, French, and didn't mind my curves, which helped me heal from the destruction Trevor left in his wake. I'm pretty fluid with lovers—again, Thailand rears its head—and I had a grand time with the ladies for the first few months.

That's how I met Saoirse—we hit it off at a bar, went to her place and discovered after one kiss that we were best friends, not lovers. She still threatens to wife me if I don't eventually find someone serious. Neither of us believe in that sort of patriarchal BS, but the threat tickles me, nonetheless.

By the time we met up again in Germany a month later, I was simply picking whatever dessert I wanted from the cart and so was she, so we cavorted around Munich throughout my entire contract like wild women. I haven't met any women who don't look like they have a stick permanently wedged in their ass in the Hollow outside of Hazel and Nelia, so that option isn't on the menu. It would simplify things immensely, I think, but also complicate them. I'll reserve judgement on that for a time when it's relevant.

Breaking out of my reverie, I look at my computer screen. Two hours ago, I brought the groceries home, peeled off my sweaty work clothes, and donned comfy stuff while I started knocking shit off my list. So far, I've emailed Nelia and Jackson, ordered most of my art materials for the studio, and cleared my Amazon list for home and office furnishings. I'm due a little physical activity before dinner.

I stand and stretch, walking to the hall closet to pull my yoga mat out. Plopping my Air Pods in my ears and my phone in the pocket on my thigh, I pad out through the kitchen towards the backyard. The landscaping here is immaculate—obviously a result of Gene and his boys keeping it over the years. Stepping onto the smooth concrete of the patio, I look out in the wide expanse, studying the direction of the sun as it sinks into the horizon. There's room on the porch past the long table, chairs, and cooking setup, but I think I'd prefer to be closer to nature.

The grass is slightly damp as I walk out into the yard, flicking my mat out in an open space between the swings and fire pit my parents put in years ago and the patio setup. That circle of fire and air was the *one* major thing I asked my parents to give me that they didn't fight me on. In fact, they loved the idea of a roaring fire pit in the autumn evenings with large comfy basket swings big enough for two placed around it. Sometimes, when my mom was home, we even sat out there together, reading in our swings by the waning light until it was too dark to see.

I'll be damned. That memory came easier than any memory has recently. Maybe it's because it's so innocuous.

Shaking my head at the ridiculousness that is my psyche, I pull out my phone and turn on my patented 'Bad Ass Bitch Mix'. I know it's weird to do yoga to loud slammin' tunes, but re-affirming my inner strength and my physical strength is what I'm after. Hence, I listen to a playlist full of women who aren't here for men's shit. With the week I've had, it can't hurt to gather my *cajones* and get tough.

I start in tadasana, feeling my breath flow as I close my eyes. As the music pumps in my ears, I move through uttanasana and into ardha uttanasana. The stretch in my back after all the lifting, carrying, and fucking is marvelous. I pause for a moment, breathing through the muscles as they ache. Not doing yoga for a week was a mistake I won't make again. I can't even imagine what would happen if I'd driven to that gym I looked up to practice my Muy Thai.

The sounds of nature filter in past the headphones occasionally as I slide my hands down my calves, walking them forward until I'm in plank position. Holding it while the muscles in my abs tighten, I open my eyes, looking out at the sunset as I breathe. Dipping to chaturanga, I hold again as my breath pushes in and out, and loud music fills my mind. My body goes to pure muscle memory as I curl my toes and push up to urdhva mukha svanasana, making my calves and hamstrings sing with the burn this time. By the time I switch to adho mukha svanasana, I'm really feeling my lack of commitment and the bloody sexcapades.

I'm gonna be sore AF when I go to bed. Maybe it'll keep me from jumping the next hot dude that bats his lashes at me and uses an infuriating nickname.

Jumping back to uttanasana, I stop to breathe again as I finish my sun salutation. I'm about to raise my arms and start my virabhadrasana sequence when a loud screech followed by a small, more high-pitched call startles me. The birds are loud enough to cut through the pounding bass of Queen B, and I turn around, putting my hand up to my eyes to shield them as I face the brightest point of light coming from behind my house.

An enormous eagle—literally the biggest damned bird I've ever seen in flight—comes swooping down into my yard. It's fucking beak is the size of a bloody bear's paw, and there is NO mistaking that this is a predator bird. Where in the seventh circle of Lucifer's whorehouse did this MONSTER come from? Is this one of the townspeople's crazy-ass companions? After meeting Zareb, I wouldn't put it past that old bitch Zelda to send her man-eating eagle after me.

Eyeing the bird carefully, I bend to pick my phone up, making certain that I don't make any sudden movements. Jekyll and Hyde are in the house, and for once, I'm glad they aren't here to mix it up with something that's spooking me. This bird has talons that look like it can kidnap *children*. I sure as hell don't like their chances if they start shit with it.

Once I'm upright, the bird tilts its head toward me, looking puzzled. Yeah, no more than me, buddy. I swipe the screen open, watching the bird as my thumb scrolls to the number at the bottom. I added Wolfie last, and given he's a vet, perhaps he will come rushing to my aid before I become this bird's Happy Meal.

It rings for an interminable length of time before he picks up, his voice muffled in my pods. Whispering low, I say, "I have a situation. There's a... very large, very hungry-looking bird in front of me. If it had scales, I'd swear it was a fucking pterodactyl. Can you help?"

There's a pause, a shuffle, and his voice is low as he responds. "Well, sugarplum, you're doing the right thing. It's not an escapee from the dino park, but since I'm currently hanging out with our resident bird expert, you're in luck."

I blink. Whistler's Hollow has a resident bird expert? What the fuck DOESN'T this damned to—Suddenly, I remember the sexy shirtless dude that was removing a redbird from the crawl space. Holy shit, THAT must be the bird expert.

Or should I say, *Dr.* Bird Expert?

Letting out a wispy chuckle, I pretend to smile at the bird, hoping it stays non-confrontational while I figure out what to do. "Um, so if Dr. McNuggets is there, could I turn on the camera and show you this thing?"

After a few laughs and some muffled sounds, Wolfie finally answers. "Of course, sugarplum! Presley says he'd be much obliged if you did."

I take my eyes off the bird—who I decide to refer to as Eurayle because if I end up having to speak to it, I'd prefer a name—to look at my screen. I swipe the video call on, looking down at the faces of the two thigh-quakingly hot dudes on the phone. They wave as if we're having a grand safari, and I almost lose my temper. I don't know what the doc sandwich is doing, but their cavalier attitude has my teeth on edge. Do they think I'm joking about the size of this monster?

"I'm flipping the camera now, you dipshits. Don't look this excited when this thing rips out my innards."

Before they can respond, I hit the camera switch button and slowly lift the phone towards the bird. Eurayle just sits on the lounge it landed on, watching me as I move like I'm trying to slide under a laser beam.

"*Holy fuck Jolene!*"

The loud wail in my ears makes me wince and sweat slides down my spine. Are they actively *trying* to get me killed? Hissing under my breath, I grind out, "What?"

Dr. McNuggies answers, his voice laced with awe. "That is *not* a pterodactyl. That is a harpy eagle. It's one of the largest raptors in the world, and extremely far from home. Don't scare it away!" I open my mouth to answer, but he cuts me off. "Get your shit on, Lucy! We're gonna go see the coolest damned bird in the *universe* at Jolene's!"

The phone clicks off, and my eyes widen.

Now I'm trapped with the largest dinosaur bird in the world—alone—waiting for two hot dudes to save me.

Could my life be normal for like... an hour?

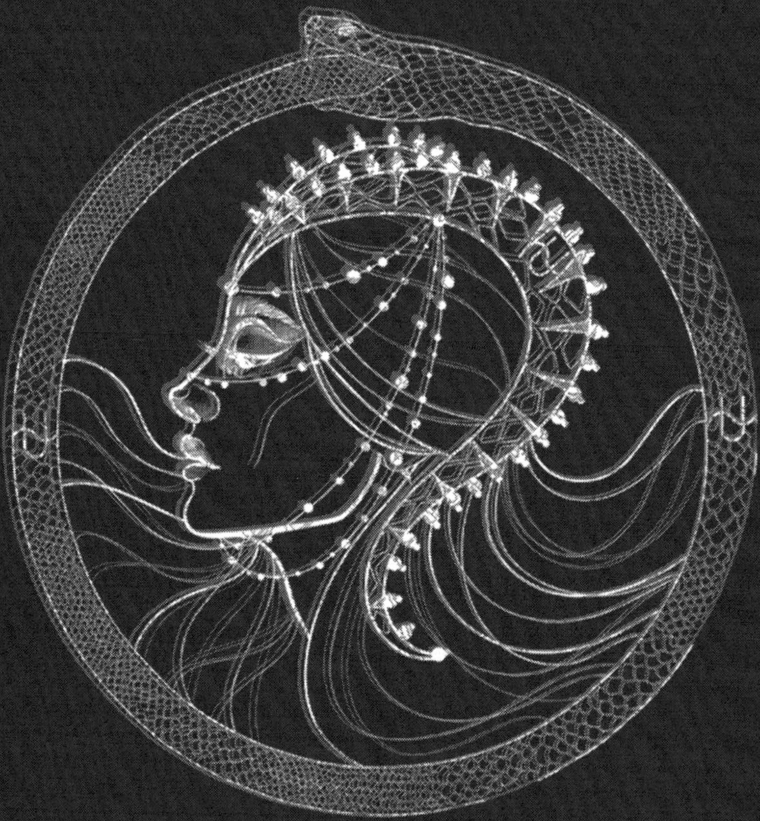

Somethin' to Talk About

Jolene

"Then the wife of the British ambassador had to let us scramble into his jet and hop to Manila, and once we hit the Philippines, we decided to party in Hong Kong for a week or two. Luckily, the passports our employers brought us *into* Thailand on weren't real, so they couldn't trace us to China. It was a *crazy* weekend," I finish, tossing a meat ball to the enormous bird.

Jekyll and Hyde burst out of the backdoor with them about fifteen minutes ago, and after much hissing, feather fluffing, and screeching, I got them all settled by feeding them. I didn't know what else to do while I wait for the docs—a story seemed like the easiest way to keep the mood calm amongst the predators.

Eurayle tosses its head as if disbelieving, and Jekyll gives a 'mow' in agreement.

When did I become the fucking wild animal whisperer? Before this week, I'd never even owned a pet. That these guys have mysteriously appeared and taken a shine to me is as much a mystery as the rest of this damned place.

Car doors slam and all three of my guests whip their heads toward the front of the house as if they plan to attack in formation. I put my hand over my eyes to shield them from the waning light, squinting as I see Hottie McBabyVet and Dr. McNuggies tromping across my lawn hurriedly.

I snort, my expression full of sarcasm as they jog over. The danger has more than passed—if it hadn't, I'd already be an eagle snack because fifteen minutes is a long-assed time in 'cornered by a wild animal' time. The cats and monster bird look at me curiously and I shrug. I don't know why they think they're white knights at this point.

"Ahoy, boys. Good thing Eurayle here likes meatballs, and the cats can somehow use doorknobs. Your rescue took longer than expected."

Wolfie flushes, rubbing the back of his neck, but Dr. McNuggies shrugs and tosses his own gauntlet back. "Given that I knew it wasn't a dinosaur and Lucy here told me it's not the first animal related scrape you've gotten into since moving back, I figured we could set reasonable rescue expectations."

My jaw drops, and I narrow my eyes at him. This pompous ass just told me whatever they were doing was more important than my safety! I untuck my legs and flip to my feet with the grace of a fighter, stalking towards him slowly. "What, may I ask, was so important that the town *doctor* saw fit to sacrifice my body to finish?"

"Sugarplum..."

The doctor smirks, holding his hand up to my little vet. "Allow me, Lucy."

I stop inches from the arrogant dick, feeling my temper spike as blood thrums in my veins. A strange sensation of righteous indignation is flooding through me, and I don't for the life of me know why I believe my safety should trump anything they had going on. I barely *know* these dudes, but I'm pissed as hell.

"Sometimes, finishing what you started is better than leaving things undone." His smirk catches my attention, and he steps closer. "You wouldn't want to be left wanting, now would you, magpie?"

It's like my entire field of vision fills with red at his implication, and every inch of my body acts on a primal instinct. There's a screech, two yowls, and a tumbling of limbs before we hit the ground. I can't focus on anything but the overwhelming drive within to teach this snarky bird watcher a lesson on who's in charge. A shiver of cold runs through me and another screech, this one louder and deeper, echoes over the hills.

The redness fades when hands slide over my arms—more hands than should be possible—and it's replaced with a hunger deep in my belly. My skin flushes, my core heats, and my legs wrap around... someone. Soft whispers fill my mind, and I can't make out what they're saying, but I know it's important. I strain to hear them, but as a cool breeze skates over my feverish body, other voices pull me back to reality.

"Sugarplum..."

A hand caresses my face, and a deep, musical tone murmurs in my ear. "Magpie, you're so hot Lucy is cooling you down. I'm gonna slide these clothes off and..."

"Yours, too," I mutter, sifting through the haze in my mind.

"Sugarplum, I don't think you realize..." Wolfie starts, his voice soft and unsure.

A low, throaty laugh escapes my lips, and if I wasn't so damned consumed, it'd surprise me. I've never made a sound like that in my life, but something is spilling inside of me. "My darling Wolfie. I know *exactly* what you were doing before you arrived. Now, hush, and take what I'm offering."

"Hell, Lucy, don't argue with the woman. Strip and be merry with us," Presley says, his eyes dancing with excitement behind the thick frames.

Wolfie does as he's asked, crawling over to my side to help me tug off the deep purple workout tank. Presley works the yoga pants down once he's bared, and whistles as he looks up at us. My current lover's tan stands out against my pale skin, and where I'm all curves, he's hard planes and muscle. Roving my gaze over him in return, the corner of my lips quirk.

"What's going through your mind, magpie? Do I not meet your standards?"

I snort, taking in the corded muscles in his legs and calves, his strong thighs, the deep 'V' at his waist, and his abs. He's absolutely *covered* in tatts under the lines of his clothes, and it must have taken years to sit for all that ink. His entire frame is a sleeve, including... I peek at his bobbing cock—yep, that, too—and lick my lips. "You'll do."

That draws a genuine laugh from Hottie McBaby vet, and his body finally relaxes. "Sugarplum says you'll do, Prez. Should we show her what exactly we'll do?"

Uh, yes, the fuck you should.

"I think she's cooled down enough that we can, Lucy," the doc murmurs, kneeling on the grass beside me. "But first, she needs to tell us what's so funny."

Reaching up, I grab his neck and tug him down with more strength than I usually apply. "If you earn it, I will."

His grin is broad as I squeeze lightly, and he wrestles away, dropping his head to my nipples. His teeth tug at the shields in all the right ways, and I know he's done this before. Neither Edgar nor Wolfie were bad, but someone who *knows* how to play with piercings is always gonna win that contest. I bury my fingers in his dirty blond locks as my back arches, and a soft laugh whispers against my side as Wolfie scoots further down.

"Y'know, sugarplum, I've decided right about here..." His mouth touches my pussy lightly and whatever he does to Presley elicits a moan that vibrates over my nipples. "... might be my new favorite place."

How in seven hells do you argue with *that*?

I don't, and neither does the doc. His fingers replace his lips as he nips around the heavy curves of my breasts. I tug on his hair, and he bites harder, making my thighs fall apart. Wolfie pushes them further and buries his face in me, his own teeth nibbling along my folds in time with Presley.

Are these dudes fucking mind readers or are they that in sync?

A pinch on my nipple brings me back and I open my eyes, looking down at my new lover with hooded lids. "You gonna tease me or fuck me, Doc?"

His eyes dance. "Little of column A, little of column B. Lucy's getting you ready. If you could control that mouth of yours, you could lie back and enjoy."

Second time this week a guy with his face in my tits has said that. I should make a t-shirt.

"Perhaps you could put it to better use?" I suggest, batting my lashes at him coquettishly. "I'd be a poor orgy host if I didn't offer my services."

Wolfie's head pops up, and he grins, his chin wet with my juices. "Point of order, sugarplum. This is a threesome. An orgy requires a few more bodies."

I almost scream in frustration when all sexy activity stops. "Thank you, McDreamy. Now, could you and McSteamy go back to making me come so we can all get off before the sun comes up?"

His answer is to dive back in so enthusiastically that my thighs shake. Presley winks and adjusts as I asked, planking over my body until I can reach for his cock. With a growl of pleasure, I tug his hips down and swallow him as far as possible as my hips grind against Wolfie's lips and tongue. I may not have expected the old six-nine, but his face meets his lover's and they do something in tandem that makes my eyes roll back into my head so far, they may never return.

Slaps and moans and rumbles fill the night with sound, and when I feel like I'm about to fall over the edge, I vow to take them with me. Scraping my teeth over his cock as I hum my way up his length, I raise my hips one more time. The wave crashes into me like a rush of warmth filling my entire body, and I lose myself in the haze that settles over my mind.

Voices buzz around me again, and I catch bits of the conversation as I smile lazily.

"... you manage the animals because she's got *cats*..."

"Do you have her? The back door is open, I think..."

Movement jostles me, but I don't open my eyes because I'm too floaty and wonderful to even take part.

"... got 'em inside. The bird is nesting..."

"... the bedroom is upstairs, right? What do you mean you don't know?"

I lift a hand to point at the ceiling, or I think I do, and chuckles echo off the marble in the foyer. At least, it sounds like the foyer. Hell, they could take me to the garage for all I know.

"... she so out of it?"

"No clue... she's a... right?"

"... no one knows..."

It occurs to me I should probably pay attention to whatever they're discussing because they've dropped to whispers, but I can't focus enough to do so.

The last thing that goes through my head as I feel bodies—

including mine—hit softness is that I hope I don't wake up alone covered in chigger bites.

That would suck.

TO BE CONTINUED IN 'RETURN TO THE HOLLOW—Misfit Protection Program Book One'

Pre-order it now!

Reviews, Print, and Merchandise

If you have enjoyed this book, please leave reviews! It helps other readers find my work,
which helps me as an indie author.

Thank you!

Reviews for Revealed in the Hollow are appreciated on the following platforms:

Amazon
Goodreads
Bookbub
StoryGraph
TikTok
Instagram
Facebook

To purchase print copies or merchandise, go to The Worlds of Cassandra Featherstone

Sneak Peek: Veiled Flame

Loser

Kat

The little blue icon on my app has been glaring at me all day, but I'm too damn nervous to open it. Everyone at Woodlawn High has been buzzing all day with their notifications and the squeals of joy and moans of despair were too much for me to take. My anxiety is through the roof—this is the moment I've been waiting for since middle school, but I can't seem to force myself to bite the billet and check.

Maybe it's because I don't have the support system most of my classmates have?

That's probably true, given I've always been a loner and I don't fit into any specific 'caste' here. It's hard to make friends when you get shuffled from foster home to foster home over the years. I've rarely stayed anywhere long enough to make a friend, much less a group of them.

I'm not delinquent or anything—the families I've been placed with just return me like a pair of pants that doesn't fit after a year or so. The caseworkers click their tongues sympathetically and hunt down a new placement, but I've never been given a reason *why* people don't want me around. One lady said I must be born under a bad sign and hell if I knew what that meant other than I'm not good enough to keep around.

It would be different, almost understandable, if I misbehaved or got bad grades. But I don't—I'm always in the top five percent of my class and I do everything I'm asked. I don't even lord my smarts over the other kids or adults. Being presentable and unassuming was something I adapted long ago to improve my probability of staying in a home long term.

Unfortunately, it never worked and though I should be a shoo-in for scholarships and acceptances galore, I can't bring myself to be rejected yet again.

So I wait for the last bell of the day, slinging my bag over my shoulder and trudging home to the latest in my temporary housing. I can't even contemplate looking at the possible heartache waiting for me in the college application system WHS insisted we use. The fear is too great and despite knowing I'll be on my own for good at the end of this year, I'm unable to risk the pain.

I hate being this way.

My court mandated therapist says it's some sort of attachment disorder that's common in foster kids, but I think that's bullshit. The problem isn't *me* not forming attachments; it's asshole adults not forming one to me. Being left at a safe haven in a fucking basket as a baby wasn't because *I* did anything wrong—again, fucking adults couldn't handle their commitments.

As usual, I arrive home to an empty house. There are two other kids who live here—Bryce and Blake—but they're at football practice. Of course, the Jamesons *love* them; they get to strut around at games because their strays are the stars of the team. I'm not mistreated, but I'm definitely an afterthought. Both of my 'parents' are still at work, so I drop my bag on the couch and head for the kitchen to get a snack:

Don't get me wrong. I *could* have been placed in far worse homes than any of the seven I've been in since elementary school. None of the ex-fosters starved, beat, molested, or abused me. They were all decent folks with jobs and houses that weren't hellholes, but they never liked me.

I have no idea why. I tried to be everything they wanted.

But when the end of each school year came, I was handed in like a textbook and off I went to some group home until the next contestant stepped up. It baffled everyone, not just me, but that's what happened every single time.

Sighing, I pull some fruit out of the fridge and grab a soda. I have homework to do and if I want to have time to work on my stories, I'll need to get it done before the house is full of people at dinner time. Bryce and Blake will have gotten messages about their applications, too, and I'd bet my pinkie toe those idiots got into some big sports school. Brett and Allison will be oozing happiness for them and I don't know if I'll be able to keep food down if I have to admit my failure when they ask.

Being eighteen sucks ass.

After I grab my books and tablet, I head down to the den. I have to give my current parents credit; they set up a very nice workspace for us to study in the converted basement. By the time they took me in, the Jamesons created a cozy room down here where the three of us could relax and do our work for school without being interrupted. It might have been more for the boys than me, but I appreciated it all the same. Desks, a couch, big chairs, and bookshelves fill the space, making it almost seem like our mini-library. They even put a small fridge for drinks and snacks in case we had to be up late to cram.

It's my favorite place in the entire house and I spend most of my time here.

I sink into the huge armchair, putting my drink and snack on the side table. It only takes a few minutes to arrange myself in the soft cushions and I pause to tug my headphones out of my pocket. Music always soothes my jagged edges and I need it to stay focused on the bullshit AP Calculus I need to keep my average up in. My course load is heavy, but I applied to tough colleges. I wouldn't have a chance to get in, especially on a scholarship, if I wasn't taking equally challenging classes in comparison to all the prep school kids.

As always, the sounds of Vivaldi carry me away as I scrawl equations on my screen and before long, thoughts of the blue notification completely fade away.

○

"Kat!"

The shouts barely register as I continue working on the problem set, gnawing on my lower lip in concentration.

"Jesus fuck, where is she? I could eat a hippo!"

"Kat!"

Thumping followed by what could pass for a stampede of elephants jerks me out of my math filled trance when Bryce and Blake come down the stairs. They smell as bad as the aforementioned pachyderm's cage, so they must have rushed home right after practice. The blond twins glare at me as if I'm the offending element despite being sweaty and covered in dirt and grass stains.

This doesn't bode well.

Usually, they're tired and hungry after practices so I'm used to cranky ass boys, but tonight, there's a light to their faces. That had to mean they've gotten their letters and dinner will be a gush fest in honor of their perfection. I'm going to need all of my strength to fake smile and nod as Brett and Allison fawn over them.

I don't begrudge them their success—not really. They work hard and play even harder on the field. It's not their fault they're the American dream teens and I'm the nerdy basement troll no one wants. But it's awfully hard living in the shadow of their bright light, especially when I'm no less intelligent or talented.

"I'm finishing the AP Calc, guys. What do you want?"

They roll their eyes at me before Blake scoffs. "It's not due until Monday. You're so hyper."

Duh. I take anxiety meds, douchebag; of course I'm 'hyper.'

"I can only be who I am, Blake." That earns me a snort from Bryce and I know it's because he thinks that's the problem. "Is dinner ready?"

"Almost. Get upstairs and set the table so we can shower—Brett's orders." Blake grins smugly.

The two of them seem to always arrange it so chores get passed to me for some half-assed reason and this is no exception. Sighing,

I put my stuff aside, fully intending to hide down here after the dinner mess is cleaned up. Likely by me, but like I said, I could definitely live in worse foster homes so I let it go. Doing some chores isn't worth risking the group home for the last few months of my high school career.

They take off running up the stairs and I wait for them to disappear before I follow suit. My phone is tucked in my pocket and I feel like it's a stone of shame I have to bear. I know once the adults make over the twins' success, they will remember me, and I'll be forced to find out what disappointment lies in wait for me. The dread weighs on me, but I head into the sunny kitchen and pick up the pre-prepared pile of plates, silverware, and napkins on the counter.

Allison looks up from the stove and gives me a half-smile, nodding as I take the dishes into the dining room. Like I said, no one is mean or horrid, they just seem...obligated. After a while, it makes it hard to waste time trying to be bright and sunny. Being reserved makes it a hell of a lot easier not to feel rebuffed when they don't pay attention to you regardless.

"Make sure you include champagne glasses for your dad and I!" she calls from the other room.

The twins definitely got acceptance somewhere big. Brett must have gotten the bubbly on the way home.

Once I set the table, I return to help Allison bring out the roast and sides. I'm a little amazed at her efficiency when it comes to getting the housework done while working full time, but I suppose it's something people with real parents get taught as they grow up. My home life has been so fractured that I haven't learned how to cook more than very basic shit from YouTube videos. That may be a problem after graduation, but I've never felt comfortable enough to ask Allison if she'd teach me. I'm sure she would try, but it doesn't feel right.

"How was school, Kat?"

I look over my shoulder, seeing Brett in the entry to the dining room. He's already changed from work and smiling, but I see the distraction in his eyes. He's waiting for the boys to come down. "It was fine. I've got a Calc test at the end of the week. I'll be studying a lot to get ready."

"Good, good. No matter what happens with applications, keeping your grades up will ensure no one pulls any offers," he says.

Those words aren't for me. They are for the two wet haired boys who just appeared behind him.

"Kat's too much of a geek to ever let her grades slip, Dad," Blake says as he pushes past his brother and drops into his usual chair at the table. "Grab me a Powerade since you're in the kitchen, mouse!"

Both Brett and Bryce stare at me and I turn around, heading to the fridge despite the fact that I was *not* closer than the other twin. Out of habit, I take two of the drinks and a soda for myself. I've been here long enough to know Bryce will send me back to get him one as well. It would feel like typical sibling stuff, but for some reason, I just *know* they do it to fuck with me. I have no idea why I feel that way, but trusting my gut has been the one thing that helped me get through all the upheaval in my life over the years. It's a good gauge for knowing when I'll get booted or if people are being earnest in their reactions.

The therapist says that's some sort of trauma induced early trigger warning shit, by the way.

After I hand out the drinks, I sit down on my side of the table and we wait for Allison to come out. Brett is at his seat at the far end of the table and the twins are punching each other as they look at something on their phones. I know where this is all going but I drop my gaze to the table, swallowing the coppery taste of fear as it courses through my body.

I'm going to be exposed and there's nothing I can do to stop it.

Read the first three episodes free on Kindle Vella: https://www.amazon.com/kindle-vella/story/B0BSTMB1X3

Sneak Peek:
Bloodthirsty

QUEEN BEE

They dim the lights in the club, and the spots click on as the curtain slides open.

It's a full house tonight in the little burlesque club off the Rue Pierre Montaine.

Chez Arc En Ciel is not well known compared to the *Moulin Rouge* or *Le Lido*, but the wealthy from both sides of the Seine gather here for shows four nights a week. If you pass the various layers of security checks to even be permitted to book a reservation, you also have to be able to afford the two thousand Euro per guest cover charge. If you don't eat or drink anything, that's all it will cost; however, that would get you blacklisted.

Intro music pumps through the speakers and I stand on my mark in the opening position. My cane is resting on the wooden boards of the stage by my front foot as I pretend to lean on it. Roars of applause echo through the room as our troupe of dancers catch the lights, sequins sparkling like diamonds when the stage lights rise. We're dressed in pinstriped black pant suits and fedoras to match the big band style opening to the song. As soon as the horn-filled intro finishes, the dance begins.

I follow the routine with precision, snapping and popping my hips to the beat as we spread out across the stage. You wouldn't know by the fake smile on my face that I'm scanning the crowd. Two fan kicks later, I've rotated past the proscenium, and I think I've found my mark. Twirling, I stop in the place I need to be for the bridge, singing along as if my life depends on it. It might, to be honest, because I need to sell my cover tonight, so no one notices me.

The Guillotine moves in the shadows, but tonight, she's in the spotlight.

My ass shakes as I dance my way through the song, swinging

the prop cane I'd replaced with one of my design. You wouldn't know by looking at it, but it's not the painted balsa the other dancers have for a very specific reason. I need it to complete the mission that forced me to spend two months in Paris working my way into this job at *Chez Arc En Ciel*. If I can't strike tonight, the surveillance, counterintelligence, and time spent building this cover are wasted because my mark is leaving for Asia tomorrow.

Tonight, the Cobra dies for his sins.

The break of the song slows the music and the dancers pour into the crowd to wiggle around the rich assholes. It's choreographed, but it's also to advertise each girl for private dances in the lounges upstairs. We're not strippers—not that there's a damned thing wrong with a woman using her body to support herself—but we do bare more skin in the closed rooms. The *laissez-faire* attitude of the owners means as long as we kick them thirty percent of the fees for those dances, they don't care what any of the girls do in the rooms. I'd find it sleazy, but the girls who work here are highly skilled performers who choose to make thousands of dollars a night rather than peanuts in some ballet troupe or chorus line.

By the time I've flirted my way to the VIP tables, the Cobra is staring intently at all of us. Spotlights pin each one of us on the floor at the bass hits, and I swivel my hips as my free hand slides down to the secret spot on my jacket. In unison, we tear the jackets off to reveal rhinestone studded bras with straps crisscrossing our waists like shibari ropes. A lift of the fedora and pop of my hip, along with the beat, draws the fierce-looking brawler's eyes directly to me. I pout prettily and stalk towards his table with the swagger of a tiny dicked asshole that owns a monster truck.

His thin lips pull back over the famed curving fangs he had implanted. Dark, glittering eyes follow every move I make as I approach, and I pretend to whip my hair from side to side as I check for his guards. They're here somewhere, but I need them to be far away so I can beat my escape before they notice. When I get within inches, I tap his leg with my cane and spin around to shake my ass in his face. The grunt of approval makes me want to heave, but I turn, holding onto the prop with both hands. My feet click on the floor in a soft shoe step as I make 'fuck me' eyes at the dirty bastard. He leans back, his pants tented as he gestures towards his lap.

Fucking gross.

I don't care about his weapons trade or what happens when people get the shit he moves. I have no clue why I have to take him out. The reason they have sentenced him to death isn't part of my contract, and I'm nothing if not a dispassionate observer of the darkest parts of human desires. Twelve years at *l'Academie* ensured I care very little about anything that isn't directly related to my ability to complete my jobs.

Sighing, I dance closer and drop onto his rather unimpressive erection and wiggle. There's plenty of cloth between us to prevent him from doing anything I'd make a scene over, so I focus on the task at hand. I slip the cane behind his head, resting the wood against his neck as I tug him forward. The move reads as playfully bringing his face to my breasts, but at the last second, I click the release built into the custom weapon. One end slides open to reveal the razor sharp garotte and before he can say a word, I yank it through.

Faint gurgling is the only noise besides the end of the song, and I carefully slide the sides of the cane together. Climbing off the nasty fucker, I put my hands on his cheeks so I can pretend to flirt with him while I arrange the head so it looks as if he's leaning back in the booth. It needs to look realistic to allow me to return to the stage with the others. When I have it settled, I back away from the booth, blowing fake kisses as I walk backwards through the crowd. I almost collide with a dark-haired guy with his collar pulled high as I head for the stage, and I roll my eyes. Whatever celeb that is trying to keep their face away from the paps is doing a shitty job of it.

The entire troupe takes a few bows and shuffles off of stage left to the wings. I exhale a sigh of relief when the next group enters on the opposite side. I haven't heard shouting yet, so I don't think the Cobra's men realize he's down. Now I take this emetic pill, have a vomiting episode, and I'll get sent home.

That's when Arabella Montaigne, the burlesque dancer, will cease to exist, and Remy Arsine Benoit will re-emerge.

I smile to myself as I chew on the tablet that will have me retching my guts out in a few moments. This is a more complex extermination than I usually prefer, and I can't leave my normal calling card behind. The Cobra's head had to remain in the booth rather than get delivered to his home in a basket.

Such a shame, that. I quite enjoy the reactions my little gifts engender when they're discovered.

Walking into the dressing room, I carefully strip my costume off, putting all the pieces in my bag. Every item in the locker room that belongs to gets placed in the duffel carefully as I wait for the effects to hit me. It won't do to leave loose ends, even if my prints have never touched a single surface in this place. My gut roils and I turn, facing one of the other dancers as the vomit finally comes. Gracelia screams like she's being skinned when I hurl on her and it's everything I can do *not* to smirk through the chunks.

"*C'est la merde!*" she shouts, running for the showers as if she's on fire.

It takes less than a minute for the owner to send me home for the night. I walk out the back door of the building with everything just as the sirens scream.

Perfect timing, as always.

I jump into the first cab I can hail, directing him to the *Hôtel de Crillon*. Their suites are the ritziest in Paris, and it's my go-to hideout when I'm here. I used to only stay in the Bernstein Suite, but some rich fuckwad purchased it six months ago. If I could track them down and beat the hell out of them, I would, but I booked my schedule until late 2025. Assassins with my skill set and accuracy are getting harder to find. They forced the old guard into retirement because they refuse to adapt to the digital age. Too many cameras, crime labs, and hackers running about to do everything Cold War style.

The future of murder for hire is millennial, people. We're old enough to be stable, but young enough to be agile with new technology. Plus, most of them are broke AF from crooked ass student loans.

It's not an issue I have, but I've been in the business since I hit double digits. You don't survive *l'Academie des Invisibles* if you haven't killed someone before the end of primary school. It's unheard of.

I was eight the first time I used the weapon that would become my signature.

Shivering, I tap on the window of the cab and bitch the driver out. He's taking a longer route than necessary to raise my fare, and I'll have his guts for garters if he doesn't knock it the fuck off. A string of curses in French erupt from him when I voice the accusation, and I slam my palm on the window with enough force to crack the plexiglass barrier. He almost drives into another car, but when he regains control, he makes the requested adjustments to our route.

We arrived at the front entrance after a few more arguments and a traffic jam around the *Champs*. I throw the euros at him in disgust, memorizing the medallion number for later. He's not worth my time, but I have quite a few contacts who might be interested in blackmailing a cabbie in town. Getaway cars are cliche in the crime world now. Most ne'er-do-wells like myself find greater comfort in anonymous taxis or ride-share accounts hacked through the deep web accessed on burner phones. If your ride doesn't know you're a villain, there's no one to flip if law enforcement comes looking.

I never look the same for any job—ever.

I will not use Arabella Montaigne as a cover in the future, and once I move to the location of my next job, I'll ensure that she meets with a terrible fate. It's a lot more work to slowly kill off my alters once I've used them, but it's also why I've never even come close to being caught. The dancer with long wavy red hair, freckles, and big green eyes will never grace the streets of Paris again after I hop a plane. She will, however, get a minor story in the paper and an obituary when I decide how she tragically dies.

The Guillotine will rise from her ashes and be reborn.

Sneak Peek: Children of the Moon

Prologue

Twenty-one years ago...

A powerful wave of apprehension hits me as we approach Claridon's house. Pausing at the edge of the forest, I wait until we can see what awaits us. The silence is deafening as we take in the wreckage of what was once the home of our dear friends.

They splintered the heavy cabin door in pieces littered around their yard like an explosion sent the shards flying. When the wind shifts, the foul stench of death and rot slams into us, making my wife gag. Lights are flickering ominously in the shattered windows and another scent—burnt food—catches the breeze as we approach.

"Cast protection before we reach the porch," I murmur.

"*Ego invoco deus ab mihi. Protego mihi ab hostili et malum.*[1]"

I nod solemnly, repeating her words to invoke our Goddess' watchful eyes on me as well. The scene in front of the house does not inspire confidence about what we will find inside.

The air is thick as we step onto the porch and another smell wafts towards us—blood. Its metallic tang invades our senses almost to the point of tasting copper on my tongue. Climbing over the debris, I look at the once cozy living area. Shredded cushions, torn drapes, stuffing, and other destroyed furnishings lie scattered around the room. When I bend to examine the destruction, I find coarse animal hairs embedded in the remnants. I pick some up to sense the aura of the creature it came from, but all I feel is death.

The bloody hoof prints puzzle me—I do not recognize them as belonging to any creature I'm familiar with. Whatever came to this house was not a normal shifter, nor was it a common magic user. The level of malice and lack of emotion concerns me. Its aura is like that of a necromancer or one of their creations.

I follow a set of heavy prints to the hallway leading to the dining area and kitchen. Swallowing hard, I prepare myself for the carnage I know will appear. The rotten food and decomposition scents are so bad I have to raise my shirt to cover my nose before I vomit.

It is certain our friends are dead; no one can lose the amount of blood that coats the surfaces and walls while staying alive.

"What made those claw marks? I've never seen such deep furrows," my wife whispers.

I shake my head, holding a finger to my lips to keep her quiet. I've never seen that type of mark, either, but we don't know if there's anyone still here. We must stay silent while we explore. The food on the stovetop is burned and has flies on it—that's the rotting smell. Wood is barely burning in the oven, just a few embers remaining, but it tells me our friends were caught unaware.

It means the malevolent being that attacked the wolves did it within the past few hours.

My heart stops when I remember their baby girl. Feray had to be here when it happened; it's the New Moon and both of her parents stay home during the start of the new lunar cycle.

"Freya, forgive me. I almost forgot the baby," I hiss at my wife.

Her eyes widen and her hand flies to her mouth. I see the tears forming as she thinks about what the condition of this place means for a defenseless infant. Together, we leave the kitchen, intent on heading back through the outer room to the stairs.

Just beyond the landing, we stumble over the body of Claridon. His corpse is mutilated, but I recognize those battered hands anywhere. He clearly put up a hell of a fight to keep the intruder from making it past him. Despite that, it ripped his chest open and his intestines are hanging out. Blood spatter decorates the once lovingly decorated walls, painting them vermillion and signaling his desperation to protect his family.

Swallowing again as I look at Imogen, I tilt my head at the trail of bloody hoof prints that lead to the nursery. We were here when they found out they were expecting, when they assembled the room, and even after Feray was born. Now the beauty of that memory has been sullied by the scene before us.

We have to be strong...

Once we're both ready, we follow the prints to the door of the baby wolf's room. The sight that greets us is horrific: it splayed Lyra out as if nailed to a cross and impaled her head on a post of the baby's crib. Blood is dripping down the whitewashed wood, making its way to the pink carpet. Dead eyes stare sightlessly at us as we hold our breath and enter. The injuries to our friend are a testament to how hard she fought to protect her child, though in the end, she also failed.

I don't want to see what this monster did to the baby we considered a sister to our child. Forcing myself to approach, I stare at the empty crib in astonishment. There's no sign of Feray, nor that it harmed her in this room. I whip my head around to look at my wife in shock.

Was this a kidnapping? Why would they kill everyone so brutally instead of simply sneaking in to snatch the baby?

My eyes dart around the room until I reach the closet. I stalk over, throwing the door wide. There's a pile of dirty linens and blankets in the bottom, which is unlike Lyra. She always kept everything tidy, so much so that we all teased her about it. Tossing the clothes over my shoulder, I dig down until I reach the floor. I call for light and my magic brightens the dark space enough for me to see a tiny seam at the baseboard.

Claridon was always paranoid, and I never understood why. We both lived simple lives in a small town of magic users and shifters, well outside the dangers of the big city. He was a master craftsman and Lyra ran a bakery; there was nothing to worry about. Humans were far away from our little town and the stench of corruption from the gangs and Councils doesn't exist in Silver Falls.

But I recognize a bolt hole when I see one, so I search frantically until I find the lever that will spring the door open. It takes several tries to successfully open the door—Claridon was top-notch at his trade—but when it swings out, I gasp.

There, wrapped in her father's shirt and Lyra's clothing, is Feray. She has the warding amulet Imogen made for her on her chest, and I realize that even while scared for their lives, Lyra and Claridon ensured the beast wouldn't find their child. Between the magic of our amulet and their scent swaddling her, the baby is hungry and tired, but safe.

I lift the tiny infant out of the hole gently, my eyes filling with tears. Her baby scent makes my heart hurt for my fallen friends and I clutch her to me tightly. It's our responsibility to take care of her now; I know that. Imogen nods when I look at her with a sad expression, then walks over to the dresser, opening a drawer. When she hands me the baby sling, I know she feels the same.

Once I secure Feray to my body, we make our way back to the stairs and head out of the house. It will need to be burned to keep that creature or anyone else from following the scent trail to our home. We don't want anyone to know Feray is alive; she will be safe with us as long as we continue to have her wear the amulet that suppresses her wolf.

Raising her with our daughter, in a new town, is the only way to keep her alive.

I didn't wake up this morning knowing I'd have to abandon my entire life and our home, but I know as surely as the sun will rise tomorrow what we must do to protect this baby. Looking down at her curiously, I ponder the situation again. A magical beast used as an assassin seems like overkill if their target was the infant. Slaughtering her family was also unnecessary—that thing could have slipped into her room and killed her before anyone knew it was there.

Lifting the magic on her amulet for a moment, I wait until

Feray opens her eyes. That's when I realize why my friends put it on her. My wife walks up beside me and runs a finger over her cheek. Her red hair looks very much like mine and as long as we keep the magic refreshed for the spell, she will look as though she is our natural daughter.

"We must pack up and move immediately," Imogen says as we walk out. "The capital city is vast, and no one knows us there. That will allow us to raise her as our own—a sister to Fiadh."

"Yes," I murmur. "I will send a message to the local council to inform them we are moving. The death of our friends and their daughter are too much for us to bear here. You simply need to keep her secret in our home until we leave."

She nods. "What about the monster who did this? Who would send it to kill a baby, and why?"

"Someone who scared Claridon enough to make a secret bolt hole in the nursery and forced Lyra to ask us for that amulet. I don't know what they were up to, but obviously, it was much bigger than our tiny town."

Imogen frowns. "We made three amulets, love. Why weren't Lyra and Claridon wearing theirs?"

"I don't know, Gen. Whatever the reason was, they took theirs off and someone powerful hunted down their daughter. Nothing is what it seems here, but we must protect Feray. We will keep her wolf suppressed for as long as possible—up to her Ascension if we can. She'll grow up and if she's destined for something bigger, she'll be able to assume that mantle when she's ready."

Taking this baby on and keeping her secret violates our coven laws; we both know it. Hiding her means we will always be on the run—we need completely new identities when we flee to the capital. It's a lifetime commitment, but the look on my wife's face tells me she's certain this is the right thing to do.

I know without a doubt that being was pure evil, and it came with one purpose: *assassination*.

Tomorrow, we begin our lives on the lam with two babies—there is no other option .

Get it now: **https://books2read.com/newmoonrisingCOM1**

---

1. I call on the gods. I protect myself from enemies and evil

About Cassandra Featherstone

Cassandra Featherstone has been writing since she could hold a pencil.

She wrote her first story about a girl picking strawberries when she was three and has been creating worlds in her head ever since. After winning multiple awards for essays, poems, short stories and a very cheesy academy romance novel in high school, they selected her to attend the prestigious Governors School for the Arts in high school.

Her love of the arts is vast: she plays three instruments and marched flute/piccolo for six years), took ten years of tap/jazz/ballet/tumbling, and sang/acted major roles in many musicals and plays. She auditioned for a slew of colleges, but selected NYU for musical theater and lived in NYC for several years while she was in the studio.

After meeting her husband, she moved back to the Midwest and eventually spawned her mini-me, affectionately known as the goblin.

She has worked in many industries, from banking to retail management and, most recently, a decade in multiple positions at an indie bookstore until COVID-19 permanently closed her educational services department.

Cassandra is passionate about literacy, but when she picked up her laptop to write her first published novel in March 2020, she focused on subjects that not only spoke to her soul, but affected many of the women she'd met throughout her twisty life path.

Bullying, PTSD, body dysmorphia, mental illness, reinvention, and claiming your space are frequent themes in her books, as well as respectful, non-fetishized representation of LGBTQIA+ relationships. Her expansion of the reverse harem genre to include various types of polycules and diverse characters with three-dimensional personalities, hopes, and dreams was less common when she first published, but to her delight, becoming a standard reader request in the current atmosphere.

Because of her personal experiences in middle and high school, Cassandra is a staunch defender of those who get targeted by those with actual or perceived power that attack those who don't.

She's also affectionately known as the Muppet for her outrageous, extroverted personality and her wacky brand of theater kid social media posts and videos.

Cassandra lives in the Midwest/South with her computer geek husband, artsy college goblin, an author dog, and five cats that Loki himself spawned. Her works include sci-fi fantasy/urban fantasy, paranormal, humorous, contemporary, and academy whychoose/polyam romances with characters over eighteen. Her books never include non-consensual elements, but feature accurate, safe depictions of BDSM and kink lifestyles.

READ MORE AT CASSANDRA'S WEBSITE OR HER FACEBOOK PAGE. SIGN UP FOR EXCLUSIVE CONTENT AND UPDATES HERE.

FIND HER ON ANY OF THE SOCIAL MEDIA BELOW AS SHE *LOVES* TO CHAT AND *NEVER* SLEEPS!

Also by Cassandra Featherstone

THE MISFIT PROTECTION PROGRAM SERIES

Road to the Hollow

Return to the Hollow

Home to the Hollow

Rejected in the Hollow

Revealed in the Hollow

Revenge in the Hollow

AUDIO OF THE MISFIT PROTECTION PROGRAM SERIES

Road to the Hollow

VILLAINS & VIXENS

Bloodthirsty (Book One)

Ruthless (Book Two)

Wicked (Book Three)

AUDIO OF THE VILLAINS & VIXENS SERIES

Bloodthirsty

Ruthless

TRIANGLES & TRIBULATIONS

Hoist the Flag (PQ)
Yo-Ho Holes (Book One)

CHILDREN OF THE MOON- WITH SERENITY RAYNE

New Moon Rising (Book One)
Waxing Crescent (Book Two)
Waxing Gibbous (Book Three)
Full Moon (Book Four)

APEX ACADEMY CAPERS

Come Out and Prey
Let Us Prey
In Prey We Trust
Eat. Prey. Love.

FAETAL ATTRACTION

Hell on Wheels (Book One)

KINDLE VELLAS

Blood on the Ice (Secrets of State U S1)
Veiled Flame (Discordia University S1)

Blood From A Stone (Denizens of the Dark S1)

The Beast Rising (complete S1-3)

Curiosity and the Kitty (The Riftverse S1)

Hell on Wheels (Faetal Attraction S1)

Rescued by Reindeer (Exile Islands S1)

Questionable Enchantment (Adventures in Tanah Cerita S1)

Forbidden Fates (Agents of the Ouroboros S1)

ANTHOLOGIES

Unwritten

Shifters Unleashed

Jingle My Balls

Love is in the Air

(Featuring 'Reunion in the Hollow' with Serenity Rayne)

Silent Night

(Featuring 'Hoist the Flag')

Snowed In

(Featuring 'O Holy, Spite')